This is the third
Finch P
(age twelve years, tw
and two d
My first diary was called
DO NOT READ THIS BOOK
My second diary was called
DO NOT READ ANY FURTHER
So no one but ME
is allowed to read them!

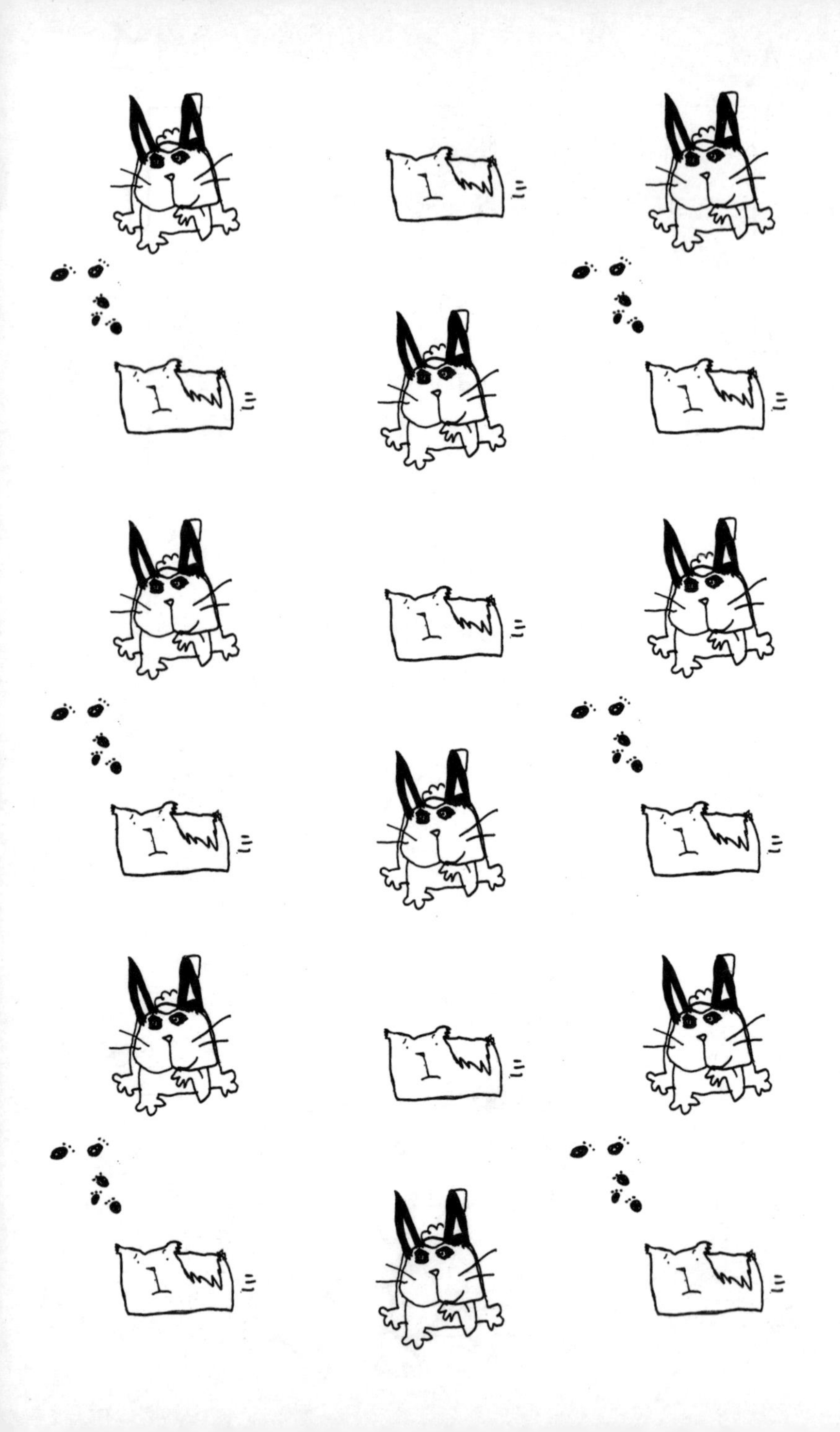

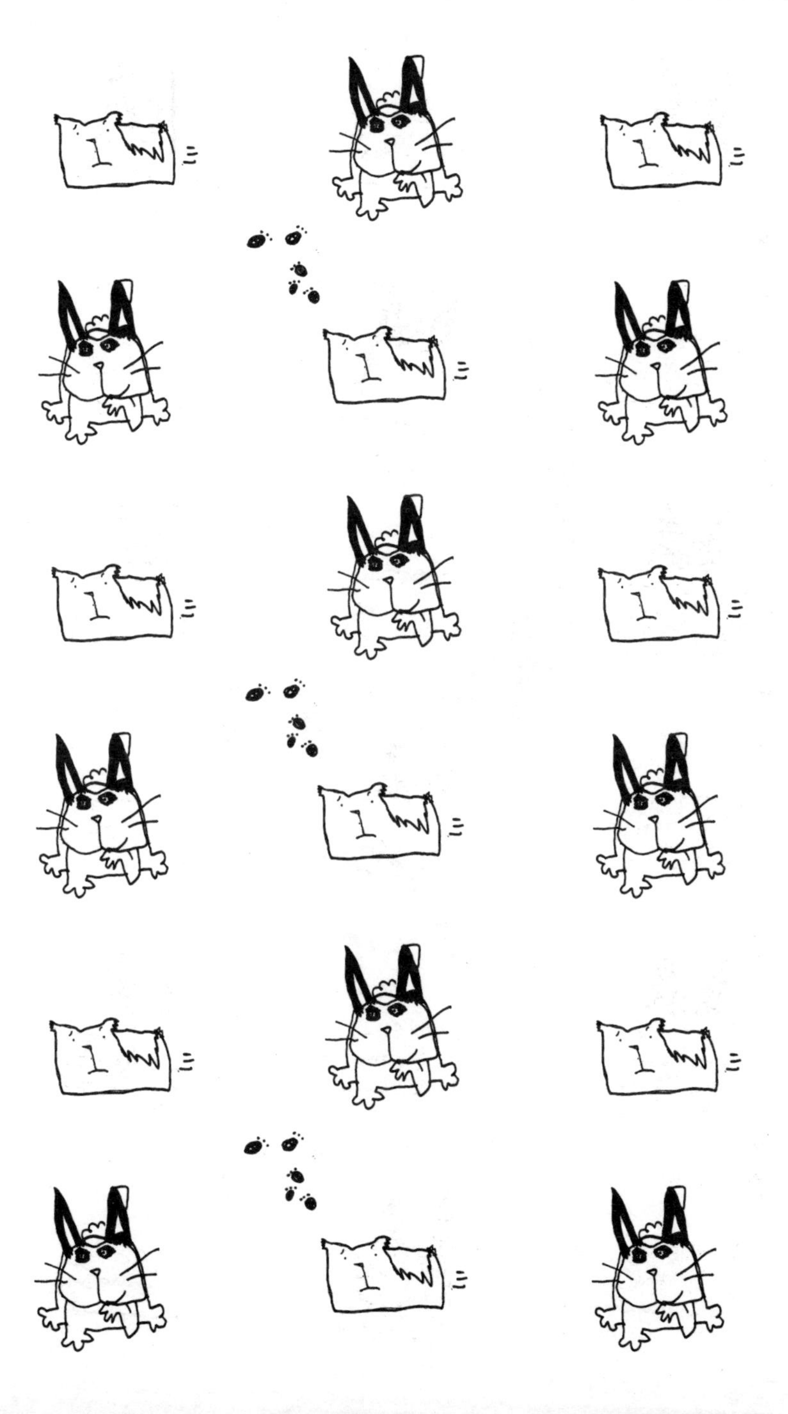

DO NOT READ OR ELSE!

Part Three of
FINCH'S TOP SECRETS* ON

Who is my dad?
Truths and lies
Boyfriends
Breaking up and making up

Lovehearts
Kissing
The Zodiac Girls

S.E.X.
Stupid smelly dogs
My scary aunt
Weddings and bridesmaids

My roly-poly pregnant mum
Stepdads
Sleepovers
Etcetera

**As revealed only to Pat Moon*

STOP!

DO NOT READ ON!

Do I make myself clear?

STRICTLY PRIVATE!

So **GET OUT** of here!

OR ELSE!

BE WARNED!

Warrior Princess
Twinkle Guinea Pig
patrols these premises
at all times!

KEEP OUT!

THIS BOOK BELONGS TO

Finch Olive Penny

HAIR – Long and dark brown.

EYES – Green.
(Jay says they have little golden flecks.)

HEIGHT – 168 cms.

WHAT I LIKE ABOUT MYSELF
Hair and eyes.

WHAT I HATE ABOUT MYSELF
My SPINDLY legs.
But I quite like wearing glasses now,
they're ***cool***
AND
I am now wearing a 32B bra!
(Which is only a ***teeny-weeny bit*** too big)
I HAVE BOOBS AT LAST!

MY FAMILY:

Mum: Debbie Penny, (age 29). She was only seventeen when she had me. She's a care worker at Greytiles Home for the Elderly.

This is Mum before she met her boyfriend Ian.

This is Mum now. Can we spot the difference? YES! She is **PREGNANT!** (four months). Not with one baby. Not with two babies...but with **THREE** BABIES! Yes! **TRIPLETS!** And we all know who's to blame, don't we? YES!

It's Mum's boyfriend **IAN TANNER!** Also known as...

Age, ancient (nearly thirty-eight).

Nolly: age seventy-three. My adopted Gran. Also known as Olive McKay (she's Scottish). Mum moved into Nolly's house when she was only seventeen and expecting me. She helped Mum through some bad times.

Biker Bill (Bill Biggins): nearly seventy-five, Nolly's boyfriend. They are getting married next Saturday and Nolly will move into Bill's retirement flat. Mum and me are bridesmaids and Ian is going to give Nolly away.

Buster Biggins: Bill's stupid smelly dog.

My REAL Dad: There isn't a photo because I haven't got one. He is a MYSTERY MAN. My mum met him at a party when she was sixteen, but she never saw him again. Much later, she discovered that she was pregnant – with me! She says I look just like him with my dark hair and long skinny legs.

This is a photo of a man that my mum pretended was my dad – until I found out THE TRUTH. But that's another story. I wonder about MY REAL dad lots.

MY MATES:

Jay: Not just a friend…but my **BOYFRIEND**. We're in the same Year Eight class at Fletchley High School. He's taller than me and looks very mature for his age, more like fourteen.

Cassie: My oldest friend…since we were three years old. We were both DEVASTATED when Cassie's mum told her that she would not be coming to Fletchley High with me but going to St Monica's School for Girls. We've both made new friends, but we have promised to STAY FRIENDS **FOR EVER! WHATEVER!**

This is me and Cass when we were eleven.

This is me and Cass a few weeks ago. Cassie has joined the GOTHIC GIRLS at St Monica's.

Kerry is my best mate at school.
Jay's best mate **Dan** is Kerry's boyfriend.

OTHER MATES AT SCHOOL:

Mia, Narinder, Sara and Sabine:

Also known as THE WARRIOR PRINCESSES.
This is us in the costumes we made for the Year Eight SHAVE RAVE DISCO.

MIA is Princess Marina,
half human and half mermaid
and she rides dolphins.

NARINDER is Princess Sapphire
with the powers of
fire and healing.

SABINE is Princess Cleo
with the powers to read minds
and change into a leopard.

SARA is Princess Amethyst
with the power of flight
and she rides a unicorn.

KERRY is Princess Astra
with the power of spring-loaded
boots so that she can leap
hundreds of metres into the air
and she also has X-ray vision.

I am Princess Zarida
with the powers of
invisibility and hypnotism.

This is our chant:
We're **warrior princesses**,
do you hear?
Warrior princesses
have no fear!
Warrior princesses
give in never,
Warrior princesses
stick together!
Our **powers** are great!
Our words are **true**!
Girls, join us now
And be one too!

And not forgetting:

WARRIOR PRINCESS
Twinkle Guinea Pig.

also
WARRIOR PRINCESS
Graemella Rabbit,
daughter of Graeme Rabbit, (deceased). Graemella was born 2nd October, but I can't have her until she's eight weeks old.

Graeme Rabbit was the most intelligent rabbit in the world. I used to tell him all my secrets. He always knew when I was feeling down and would nibble my toenails to make me laugh. He died on 4th September, age four years and two weeks. He was best friends with Twinkle Guinea Pig and they shared a hutch together. Twinkle looks so lonely by herself and keeps looking for Graeme, squeaking, *Where are you? Where are you?*

Saturday 20th November

9.05.

*He **kissed** me*   **He **kissed** me**

*JAY **KISSED** ME!*

He kissed me!

Under the stars!

What a PERFECT way to begin my third diary. It happened at the Year Eight sponsored Shave Rave disco last night! Miss Moody, (my fave teacher), helped us organise it to raise some money for a hospital scanner because there's a girl in my class called Mia who got cancer. Mia and her mate Narinder used to be deadly ***enemies*** of me and my mate Kerry – but now we are ***friends.***

OOOOPS!

I keep going all tingly just remembering Jay's *kiss*. And this is how it happened! Jay and me were dancing, but it was so hot in the school hall that we went outside to get some fresh air and cool down. We sat on the wall, holding hands. The sky was full of twinkling stars. I was staring up at them when Jay leaned towards me...and his lips touched mine.

And he KISSED me. And it was so, so

...**SORRY**. Can't think about anything else but Jay at the mo. I need to do some swooning...

9.20. Jay just phoned! My tummy went all fluttery when he spoke! He's got such a cool voice.
He said, *What do you want to do then?*
I said, *What d'you mean?*
He said, *I really fancy you, you know.*
ME: *Yeah?*
JAY: *Yeah.*
ME: *Did you like my warrior princess costume?*
JAY: *Yeah. It knocked me out.*
ME: *Do you love me then?*

JAY: *Yeah. Do you want to be my girlfriend?*
ME: *No way! Only joking!*
JAY: *Yeah?*
ME: *Yeah!*
JAY: *What are you doing?*
ME: *I was lying on my bed thinking about you!*
JAY: *Say you love me, then...*
ME: *I can't...*
JAY: *Why not?*
ME: *Because certain nosy people are earwigging every word I say.*
JAY: *You mean your mum and Ian?*
ME: *Correct. And Nolly too.*

THERE IS NO PRIVACY IN THIS HOUSE!
I **desperately** need a mobile phone! But Mum says it would cost too much. I'M GOING TO MEET UP WITH JAY – at the Mall. JAY IS NOW MY OFFICIAL **BOYFRIEND!**

9.40. Kerry phoned.
KERRY: Guess what! Dan kissed me! He even kissed my bald head!
ME: WOW! Guess what?
KERRY: What?
ME: Jay kissed **me!**
KERRY: Double wow!

Kerry's coming over then we're meeting up with Jay and Dan in the Mall. She wants me to decorate her bald head with pants. Ooops! I mean **paints!** Kerry had this gorgeous black, glossy shoulder-length hair before she had it chopped and shaved off last night. But she does have a very nice shaped head. She's got £91.76 promised in sponsor money so far. I couldn't bear to watch her hair coming off (except by peeking through my fingers!).

17.40. Kerry looked AMAZING today! I used pink and gold body paints to make swirly patterns all over her head. People kept staring but she didn't care. She says it makes her feel like a **wild child**. Jay bought me a brooch in the shape of a bird. I shall wear it 24/7. It's like we're **engaged** or something! Kerry was a bit jealous of my brooch and kept hinting to Dan that she would JUST ADORE one of the ladybird bracelets, but he'd spent most of his money on her triple chocolate milkshake with marshmallows, two choc flakes, banana and cherry sauce. It cost £3.95! So he bought her a sparkly hairband reduced to 25p, which was very useful for a bald person. NOT! She wore it on her finger instead, flashing it around saying, *Look! Look! We're engaged!*

I bought some really pretty scented candles from Pound City for Nolly and Bill's wedding present. She'll need them. Bill's dog Buster has a serious farting problem. Can't afford any more. Have spent most of my money sponsoring people for the Shave Rave. I've only got 32p left. Don't know how I will manage when Nolly moves out. She gives me pocket money for doing jobs like shopping, Hoovering and ironing. She won't need me now that she's got Bill.

19.25. I just walked in on Mum and Ian having a passionate snog in the kitchen! Cringe-cringe! I mumbled, *Ooops! Sorry!* And made a speedy exit. A few minutes later they followed me to the sitting room, holding hands and with soppy grins on their faces.

Ian said, *Finch? What d'you think about your mum and me getting married?*

I was gobsmacked. But I played it cool, saying, *Don't ask me. It's up to you two.* But it wasn't what I was thinking. I was thinking, What! **Help!** I don't know! I don't want that! Do I?

And Ian said, *That's great, Finch, because we've just been talking it over, but we want you to be happy about it.* Then he went down on one knee in front of Mum, took a ring from his pocket and said, *Debs, will you marry me?* Mum went all emotional, smiling and blubbing at the same time and sniffing, *Yes! Yes! I will!* Then she gave a little gasp, and clasped her tum, squealing, *I think I just felt the babies move!* So Ian and me had a feel and **we felt them too!** Her tum is huge already, which is not surprising with three babies in there.

Next thing, Mum was hugging me and sniffing. *Oh, Finch. Thank you, love! Weren't sure how you'd feel about it. You really don't mind?* And she looked so happy and smiley that I tried to look happy and smiley too, even though there were all these **worry clouds** floating in my head. Ian had planned it all secretly. He had secretly booked the wedding at the registry office without telling Mum! And it's going to be the same day as Nolly's wedding!

I asked him, *But what if Mum had said no.* He said, *No chance! I'm irresistible!* Which just goes to show what a bighead he is. We all trooped upstairs to tell Nolly and celebrated with Nolly's ginger wine. Now I'm feeling all mixed up and even more emotional and a bit squiffy from the ginger wine too.

21.50. In bed. I've pinned my bird brooch onto my jim-jams.

WORRY LIST

How do I really feel about Mum and Ian getting married?

REASONS AGAINST:

1. It means that Ian will probably be around FOR EVER.
2. He could grow **EVEN MORE** BOSSY AND ANNOYING.
3. He can be SO finicky sometimes.

Can I put up with:

4. His singing and bounciness?
5. Ditto his very smelly trainers...
6. ALSO, living with someone who is

an EXPERT ON **EVERYTHING** can be very depressing.

7. **AND what if it doesn't work out?**

I do not want Mum getting hurt again.

REASONS FOR:

1. I think Ian really does love Mum.
2. I know that Mum really loves him.
3. We get on OK-ish most of the time – which is very surprising 'cos at first I HATED HIM **so MUCH!**
4. He makes Mum happy.
5. If Mum's happy it makes me happy.
6. We'll be a proper family.
7. I don't actually hate him any more.
8. I'll have a dad.
9. I think it would be better for the triplets to have a mum and dad that are married.
10. It's what Mum wants.
11. I've had a long talk with Nolly about them and she thinks Ian is just right for Mum.
12. He's good at fixing stuff, like my bike brakes, hair tongs, crimpers etc.
13. I've got used to him. It's weird, but I think I'd sort of miss him if he wasn't around. And I never thought I'd be saying that! He drives me nutty sometimes but that's probably quite normal. Kerry's always on

about how her dad treats her like she's still five years old.

So, that's thirteen points FOR them getting married and only seven points AGAINST. Looks like **MUM AND IAN GETTING MARRIED wins** by six points. It's still VERY SCARY though.

Sunday 21st November

11.45. Little Graemella Rabbit is now mine, all mine! Dan brought her round this morning. Jay and Kerry came too. She is eight weeks and five days old. (Graemella, not Kerry.) Graemella is SO **BOSSY!** Poor little Twinkle Guinea Pig was nibbling at some lettuce when Graemella head-butted her out of the way and wouldn't let

her near it, so we've put them in separate hutches and runs till they get used to each others' smells by sniffing through the wires. I will train Graemella to be a house rabbit, like Graeme was. But I think it's only fair that I make a fuss of Twinkle first. She was so spooked by Graemella that she just crouched, shivering in the corner of the hutch. She's sitting on my lap right now, but keeps looking around in a nervous twitchy sort of way as if Graemella might suddenly pounce.

Got to go now. It's Biker Bill's seventy-fifth birthday today. He's taking us for a pub lunch. I've made him a card. It's my artistic impression of his dog Buster riding the motorbike and Bill sitting in the sidecar. My present is a box of breath fresheners for dogs.

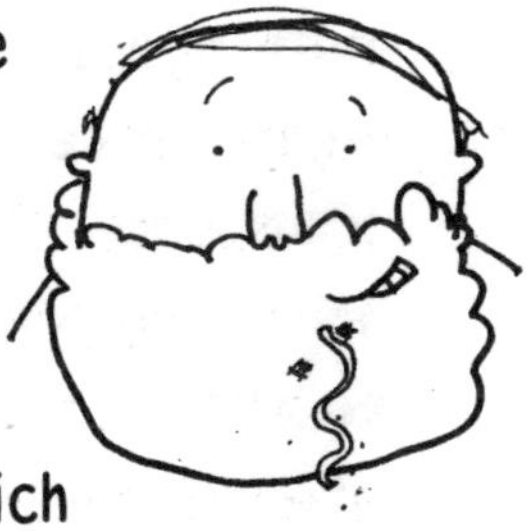

16.25. Had vegetarian toad in the hole and blackcurrant cheesecake. Yummy. Or it would have been, if I hadn't been sitting opposite Bill. He kept getting his spaghetti caught in his beard, which was very off-putting. He liked his card though. He said he's going to frame it! Had to change my skirt 'cos Buster slobbered all over it. Bill says he only dribbles on people he likes.

Twinkle keeps darting under my bed and out again. **She is SO cute!** Today she's wearing a mini nappy invented by yours truly from a panty liner and some old doll's panties. Not one guinea-pig poo anywhere! SUCCESS! A poo-free bedroom!

22.55. Kissed my bird brooch and pinned it back on pyjamas. Will wear it to school tomorrow under my sweatshirt, close to my heart.

Monday, 22nd November

16.50. Had whole school assembly. TRULY CREEPY. So many SKINHEADS! Mr Curtis and Mr Jones (Kerry's dad – and our Maths teacher!). Not that he had much hair anyway, just bits of fluff. Loads of skinhead kids too. The total raised so far is...DEE-DAH!! £627.39 – AND we'll have more after Friday, when we do the sponsored WEAR-A-HAT-OR-WIG-TO-SCHOOL. Spent all our breaks teaching millions of girls the warrior princesses dance. They want to join our group. We explained that it's an exclusive club and the words, *Join us too*, only count for the Shave Rave. They should go and invent their own stuff! Kerry was flashing her engagement hairband ring around all day.

21.30. I cannot BELIEVE that I'm on my THIRD diary! **Eight things on my WISH LIST in diary number two came true.**

1. Nolly recovered from her heart attack and she's back home from hospital.

2. She hadn't gone GAGA like we thought when she kept going walkies and disappearing. (She was having secret meetings with her new boyfriend Biker Bill!)
3. I know she hasn't started smoking again because I've checked her flat upstairs for ciggie smells.
4. I'm getting on OK at Fletchley High School and made new friends.
5. Ian (Mum's live-in boyfriend) still winds me up a little bit sometimes and he's too bouncy. Also, his trainers stink! But even though he drives me bananas sometimes, I think he really does love Mum and Mum loves him. Also he talked Mum into letting me have one of Jay's guinea pigs (Twinkle).
6. Me and Kerry have made friends with Mia and Narinder – even though we were **deadly enemies** at the start of term.
7. The spot on my nose disappeared.
8. And...TA-RAH! JAY KISSED ME!

NEW WISH LIST

1. I wish that Mia's cancer does not come back.
2. I wish that Nolly and Biker Bill will be very happy.
3. I wish that Biker Bill would give Buster

a bath, some breath freshener and something for his farting habit.

I'm amazed that Nolly puts up with it! She's very fussy about smells. I asked her about it but all she said was, *Slowly-slowly-catchy-monkey*, and tapped the side of her nose. Whatever that means. She says she has a secret weapon up her sleeve. All I could see was a bony old arm with lots of freckles. Going shopping after school tomorrow with Mum to look for our bridesmaids' gear. We don't want anything too twee. Mum wants an outfit that she can wear for her own wedding and also as her bridesmaid's outfit for Nolly's wedding.

Tuesday, 23rd November

17.35. The only thing Mum could find to fit over her bump was a pink maternity dress and a pink and black flowery poncho. My bridesmaid's gear is **FABULOUS!** I shall be wearing a black layered gypsy skirt with pink flowers, a tight pink velvet jacket and shiny pink ballet type flatties. We have these really cute matching headbands with pink daisies, feathers and pearls. Called in at Cassie's on the way back to show her. Cassie's mum started on with, *If only you would wear pretty things, darling, instead of looking like a vampire.* (Cassie is going through her **Gothic** phase.) Cassie grunted, *Yeah, well, I'm not a bridesmaid, am I? Not unless Dad gets married to **his girlfriend!***

We went up to her room where she tried on my wedding gear. The jacket was much too tight because she is now 36C bra size! But she is nearly thirteen. She looked amazing and pranced about in it like she was a film star at a film premiere, saying *Sorry! No autographs!* And blowing kisses at her fans. She showed me her wedding present for Nolly, which is **more** scented candles because she remembered me saying how smelly Buster is. They're from that posh shop, Mango. They cost £20! Cass and me have been friends since we were three so Nolly is a sort of gran to her as well.

18.40. ANOTHER MAJOR NEWSFLASH!

PLANS FOR DOUBLE WEDDING FINALISED

♡ Nolly marries Bill Biggins ♡

♡ at 10.30 at St Matthew's Church. ♡

Mum and I will be her bridesmaids.

♡ Mum marries Ian Tanner ♡

♡ at 14.30 at the Registry Office. ♡

Nolly and I will be Mum's bridesmaids and Ian will give Nolly away. Bill will give Mum away. Afterwards there'll be a double reception at the Victoria Hotel – which Bill is paying for. ALSO, – Nolly's WEDDING PRESENT to Mum and Ian is a **honeymoon weekend** in Brighton! Aunt Beryl, (one of Nolly's six sisters, all coming to the wedding), will stay over with me while they're away. I've not met Aunt Beryl yet, only Aunts Maggie and Dora and they are very nice. Nolly is their big sister. I'm allowed to invite Jay, Cassie, Kerry and Dan to the reception. Nolly and Bill will be going to Majorca for their honeymoon. But I don't want to think about that.

19.50. Bill and Ian and his mates are busy packing and moving Nolly's stuff into Bill's flat. There's no room for her furniture at Bill's so she's leaving it for us.

WISH 4. I wish that Mum and Ian will be very happy.
WISH 5. I wish that Ian does NOT get the idea that just because he's my stepdad he can tell me what to do!

Wednesday 24th November

16.50. Me, Jay, Kerry and Dan were on rota duty in the W.Y.P? office at lunchtime today. W.Y.P? stands for the WHAT'S YOUR PROBLEM? Website, invented by me, Kerry, Jay and Dan. We thought it would be a good idea for Year Eights to have our own website where kids could chat about their worries or problems and get advice from other kids. It's been going for a while now and it's **so popular** that Years Nine and Ten are using it too. UNFORTUNATELY lots of them want to help run it. (Take it over, more like.) Even more unfortunately Miss Moody thought this was a **good idea.** So now we have to put up with pushy bossy-boot Year Nines and Tens who think they know it all and treat us like infants. There were loads of Year Eight messages about the Shave Rave. Everyone wants another one!

STOP PRESS! Graemella Rabbit has just done her very first poos in her litter tray! I put it in the corner of my room and sprinkled some of her poos from her hutch into the tray to give her a teeny-weeny clue of what it is for. She looked at me, and then the tray, hopped in and did some poos and a wee-wee!! A few poos missed the tray, so I put them in for her. She had this very intelligent look on her face as if she understood perfectly. Gave her some Rice Krispies as a reward. I think she's even MORE intelligent than her dad Graeme was! The Shave Rave total has now reached £891.25! We've got the sponsored WEAR-A-HAT-OR-WIG day at school on Friday.

Thursday 25th November

8.05. This is my VERY LAST THURSDAY as the daughter of a single parent, or as a fatherless child. Spoooooky!

16.45. Kerry and I got birthday invites to Sara's thirteenth birthday party on Sat 4th December. It's going to be another warrior princess sleepover.

19.20. Just finished making my wedding present for Mum and Ian. It's SO brilliant that I want to keep it. I bought a wooden photo frame from Pound City which I'VE PAINTED in *coral pink glitter* NAIL VARNISH, and stuck little gold stars all around the frame. Nolly took some photos of Mum and Ian for me at the pub on Bill's birthday. Can't wait to see them and choose the best one for the frame.

Friday 26th November

8.10. Sponsored WEAR-A-HAT-OR-WIG day at school today. I've got £16.49 in sponsor money so far. All of us **warrior princesses** will be wearing our warrior princess sparkly wigs.

17.05. Almost **everyone** wore a hat or a wig at school today. Mrs Bloom, the school secretary, looked **truly scary** in her red CHER wig. It's not an attractive look with so many wrinkles. Everyone was in a good mood, like it was the end of term or something. Mr Morris, our class tutor, wore a Vulcan pointy-eared hat. At register

everyone had to answer 'Aye Aye Mr. Spock'. I always thought he was a weirdo. Now I know for certain. Jay wore his *Cat-in-the Hat* hat, and Dan wore his red and white Arsenal hat. Unfortunately there was a bit of a scrap between some of the Arsenal and the Chelsea supporters, which Mrs Enderby broke up with one look of her beady eye, and they were sent off to the playground to do litter-picking duty. She must be the only person who can still look scary when wearing a Noddy hat. Her bells were jingling like mad.

I think it would be an **excellent idea** to have a wear-a-hat-or-wig day twice a term. It put everyone in a happy mood – except for Mr **Grumpy** Sowerbutts. He was the only teacher who wouldn't take part! Narinder didn't wear her warrior princess wig. Instead she wore a sun hat covered in paper butterflies, which she'd made herself. She's mad about butterflies. But Mia was really foul to her. She said, *That*

hat's a big no-no with your nose, Narinder. It makes it look enormous!

I gasped, *Your nose is fine, Narinder! Mia! How can you say that?*

She giggled, *Yeah! Fine if you're a horse!* We all looked at Narinder but she just shrugged, like she was saying, *It's O.K. I'm used to it. She doesn't mean it.* When Mia was ill with cancer, Narinder used to act like she was Mia's bodyguard. Kerry and me used to be **dead scared** of Narinder! But she's not like that at all. She's quiet and kind. We reckon that Mia bosses her about.

I asked Kerry how much pocket money she gets. **She got £15 last week!** When I told Mum she snorted, *You must be joking!* I'm going to do some research and find out what my other mates get. Showed Mum the contents of my purse: seventeen pence, a bus ticket, a photo booth snap of me and Jay and my lucky glass pebble, but got no sympathy at all!

17.40. Nolly's just given me the photos she took of Mum and Ian for me. They are rubbish. Had to pretend to like them 'cos

I didn't want to hurt her feelings. Mum looks OK-ish in one, but her eyes are closed. The second has Mum looking nice but Ian has red leering eyes. The third one has the top of Mum's head missing and the fourth has Mum with a lovely smile but Ian is scratching his armpit. Oh well, it will have to be photo number four. At least they both have heads and eyes, and Ian scratching his armpit is quite typical.

17.55. I tried colouring Ian's red eyes in with a felt-tip pen. Now he looks like a **green-eyed bug**. VERY SCARY.
My very last day as a fatherless child.
Nolly's very last night in this house. Sob! Sob!

Saturday, 27th November

7.05. Had a horrible nightmare of the triplets being born at the registry office as green-eyed bugs.

TWO WEDDINGS TODAY!

10.30. Nolly marries Bill Biggins at St Matthew's Church.

14.30. Mum marries Ian Tanner at the Registry Office.
16.00. Double reception party at the Victoria Hotel. I have decided to wear my hair loose and crimped.

20.25. Mum and Ian, and Nolly and Bill are **honeymooning** now and I am all alone at home with Aunt Beryl and Buster. Aunt Beryl is watching a video of *Murder on the Orient Express.* Buster is sprawled over the sofa, even though his giant dog bed is taking up most of the carpet! I am perched on the stool.

Aunt Beryl is not a bit like Nolly. She's sort of square with muscly arms and legs and very short curly white hair, a bit like a poodle's. I think Buster is a bit scared of her. I don't blame him. I am too!

I'm feeling all mixed up. Part of me is **fizzing and bubbling** because it's been such a brilliant day. Nolly had organised line-dancing

and Scottish reel dancing at the reception. Me, Jay and Cassie and Kerry got a bit carried away, whooping and stomping non-stop and we all got a bit sweaty, which is not an attractive feature for girls. Had to keep dashing to the Ladies to cool down. Lots of Ian's relations were there. (His mum and dad are a bit weird!) Another part of me is feeling **sad**. Why am I feeling sad? I think it's because everything is changing. Nolly won't be living with us any more so I won't be able to escape upstairs to Nolly in her flat when I'm in a strop with Mum or Ian. There's also a big part of me which is feeling left out and **lonely**. Mum and me have never been apart for a whole weekend. And there's still another bit of me, which is **scared**, because I know nothing will be the same again. I wish I could bring in Twinkle or Graemella for a cuddle but they might get chewed to death by Buster, and I've seen what Buster did to Bill's slippers!

♡ ♡

And now, over to our official **wedding** correspondent, Ms Penny, for a full report.

♡ ♡

Nolly McKay, attired in a glamorous pink trouser suit with matching hat, waved from the sidecar of Bill Biggins's famous Panther 600 motorbike, as it made its way to St Matthew's Church, escorted by a convoy of Bill's biker mates. People **cheered** the happy couple as the procession drove along the High Street. The wedding ceremony was followed by a wedding breakfast at the Victoria Hotel. At 14.30, the same wedding party met at the registry office for the wedding of Deborah Penny and Ian Tanner. The bride wore a stunning ensemble of a pink maternity dress and matching poncho. Many of the groom's family, including the groom's parents, **Ron and Brenda Tanner**, travelled from Liverpool to attend the wedding. Brenda is very large and Ron is not. The bridesmaid, Miss Penny, a vision in pink and black, performed her duties **exceptionally** well, supplying emergency tissues to both grooms and brides who got a bit emotional. The reception took place at the Victoria Hotel where a buffet supper was served. Bill and Nolly led the line-dancing and Scottish reels. Finch Penny was kept busy fetching vol-au-vents for Brenda, who informed her that she could call her and Ron Nanny and Gramps. (**No way**, Jose!) The bridesmaid's best friend, **Cassandra Jane Owens**, was heard to comment, *The only reason I shall ever get married is so that I can have a line-dancing wedding like that.*

20.55. Alone in my room. My first night as a stepchild. I am worn out by listening to Aunt Beryl going **on and on** about dogs. She is mad about them! She says, *They dinna smoke, they dinna drink and they never answer back. Aye, ye know where ye are with a dog.*

I told her, *Yeah, I know where I am all right! Sitting as far away from that dog as possible because of his stinky breath!*

She said, *Och! That's one of the reasons why I'm here, lass. And it's time we made a start with him. First he needs to learn some rules.* She ordered him off the sofa, but he just yawned and scratched himself. She had to bribe him off with dog biscuits. Then she forced me to help her carry in the kitchen chairs which she piled onto the sofa and armchairs. This is her crafty plan to stop Buster sitting on the furniture. Any more of this and I'll end up with muscles like hers. Buster looked dead fed up. I don't blame him. I am too!

21.20. I can't get to sleep because of Buster howling from the kitchen. Aunt B. has shut him in there to teach him that, *He canna have the run of the hoos!* Also I'm feeling bit sad. I'm all alone with a **smelly** dog and a **mad** aunt. **Everything is changing!** And I don't like it! I think this pen is running ou..

Have found another pen. And guess what else I found? The photo of my dad! Actually, it's not *really* my dad. It's the photo of a man that Mum PRETENDED was my dad, and until I was twelve years old, that's what I believed! It all began when I was little, about three years old, and I asked Mum why I hadn't got a dad. She didn't want to tell me the truth, which was that she got pregnant by a boy she met at a party, and never saw again! So, she made up a story that she met my dad when she was working in Nolly's café, and that he was a student who was working during the holidays at a nearby building site. She got to know him because he came to the café every day. He asked her out and they fell in love and planned to get married. But one day some scaffolding collapsed on him and he was killed. She told me his name was Tom Kellogg. I found out later that this was mostly **BIG FIBS**.

THE TRUTH is that my dad was a boy she met at her friend's sixteenth birthday party and never saw again. His name really was Tom, but she never found out what his surname was. When I asked her one morning at breakfast what his surname was, it took her by surprise. She panicked a bit and she said the first name that popped into her head – Tom Kellogg. (There was a box of cornflakes on the table at the time.) Soon after the party, Mum ran away from home. It wasn't her real home because both her parents had died and she'd been living with her aunt and uncle. They were not very nice. In fact they were really horrible to her, especially her uncle, who was a **bully** and often hit her. She knew he wouldn't let her go to the party, so she'd sneaked out, but he found out about it and punished her by locking her in her room after school and at the weekends. She decided that she couldn't take his bullying any longer and when the chance came, she ran away, ending up in Fletchley (where we still live). She got a room in a hostel and a job in a café. And that's how she met Nolly! Because it was Nolly's café that mum got a job in!

Mum didn't realise she was pregnant till

much later. It was a massive shock for her when she found out! She was all alone in the world without friends or family. Nolly felt sorry for her, so she invited Mum to stay with her till she had the baby and got herself sorted. And that baby was ME! And we're still here! And that's how Nolly became my adopted gran! Nolly never had children so we are her family now.

The weird thing is that I do look a bit like the man in the photo that Mum pretended was my dad! He's got long skinny legs like me and the same dark hair. He's sitting on a motorbike. It was an even BIGGER SHOCK when Mum told me THE TRUTH! I had been secretly trying to trace my dad by going to the library and searching through the telephone directories for anyone with the surname Kellogg – **but there wasn't a single one!** It was all a waste of time. I think about my dad lots. He's out there somewhere but he doesn't know that I exist. I wonder what he would think of me? One thing's for sure, it would be a **big surprise** for him to discover that he has a twelve-year-old daughter! How old would he be now? He would have been somewhere between sixteen and twenty-ish when Mum met him – that would make him about twenty-eight-ish to thirty-two-ish now.

REASONS FOR TRYING TO FIND MY DAD:

1. I need TO KNOW!
2. I have his genes in my blood.
3. It's only natural to want to know.
4. He has a right to know about me.
5. Maybe he has sons but longs for a daughter.
6. Maybe his sons would like a sister.
7. If he has a daughter she might be longing for a sister (**half sister** actually).

(**I WOULD LOVE TO HAVE A SISTER!** We could swap clothes and stuff.)

WISH 6. I wish that I can find my dad.
WISH 7. I wish that he has a daughter so that I can have a sister.

Sunday 28th November

7.12. Aunt Beryl-the-Bossy just marched into my room and ordered, *Come along, girl! UP!* I think she has mistaken me for a dog.

7.19. Aunt B. is back again. She says *WE HAVE THINGS TO DO.* She must be mad.

Anyway, I need at least two more hours sleep. Then I have plans to go round to Jay's.

7.45. Forced to get up and go to corner shop for cooking foil. Well at least it looks like there'll be roast chicken for dinner. Yum yum! Also had to put up with Buster jumping up, scratching and whimpering pathetically at the kitchen window while I was trying to eat my cornflakes. This is because Aunt B. shut him out in the garden. She says that he's got a lot to learn. **Firstly**, he is NOT a human. **Secondly**, he is a DOG. **Thirdly**, humans are the BOSSES, not the dogs, which means he has to wait till the humans have finished their breakfast before he can have his.

8.50. A mad person is covering all the chairs in the sitting room with the cooking foil! The kitchen chairs are back in the kitchen, thank goodness, so at least I didn't have to eat my breakfast standing up! Aunt B. says the foil will stop Buster sitting on the chairs because dogs don't like the sound or feel of kitchen foil. I told her that this human being didn't like it much either and where was I supposed to sit then? She said, *Well lass, I shall be* *needing you to do some sitting in Buster's dog bed in a wee while.* **UH?**

9.10. Made an emergency phone call to Jay. He's coming over. All day on my own with Aunt B. would be tooooo scary!

9.40. Me and Jay just found Aunt B. sitting in Buster's dog bed, reading her newspaper!

She is definitely **BARKING MAD**. Ha ha. Buster looks dead worried. Aunt B. says it's all part of his retraining programme. He must understand that **HUMANS are the TOP DOGS, NOT him. Dogs can only go where we humans allow them to go.** Then she pinned up a duty rota for me and Jay to do dog-bedsitting, until Buster learns that lesson.

9.50. I am writing this in Buster's dog bed as it is my turn for dog-bedsitting duty. It's **really** comfy. I think I would like one for my room. I could have meetings in it. You could squeeze in at least four people. Or just me and Jay! Buster's looking at me with a dead miz expression and keeps whimpering.

10.05. One of my new trainers has gone missing. I bet Buster has pinched it. He's getting his revenge on me for sitting in his bed. Jay is dog-bedsitting now.

10.40. Aunt B. has gone walkies with Buster so I have put Twinkle into Graemella's run to see how they buddy up. Gave them some carrots to keep them busy. Graemella looked a bit grumpy at first and pinched some of Twinkle's carrots, but she didn't head-butt Twinkle like the first time. Will put them together for a little while every day but watch them very carefully. I have told Graemella that I will be extremely cross if I catch her menacing Twinkle!

21.05. In bed. **EXHAUSTED!** Me and Jay forced to work ALL DAY! We had to help Aunt B. give Buster a bath. (**Two** baths actually, because he escaped the first time and hid under the sofa.) Aunt B. cunningly enticed him out with a trail of doggy nibbles. He looked up at her with this soppy **adoring** expression **and** let her take him back to the bathroom! He even let her **brush his teeth!** He is a different dog. Well, the same dog, but different. It's nice not to have to hold your breath every time he comes near. Aunt B. says you have to know who's the boss. With Bill it's the wrong way round – Buster is the boss. But Nolly doesn't want to hurt Bill's feelings by complaining, so it's Aunt B's wedding present to them. I think Aunt Beryl must be the secret weapon that Nolly was talking about. Buster is lying at her feet, gazing at her adoringly. **SPOOKY**.

Still haven't found my trainer. Didn't even get a roast chicken dinner, just beans on toast. It had a dog hair in it. **EUGH!** Couldn't eat a *single* bean!

21.30. Thinking about my dad again.

REASONS FOR NOT TRYING TO FIND MY DAD

1. Mum would go ballistic if she knew I was even thinking about it.
2. Ian would take Mum's side and lecture me

to **death** in that patient-and-understanding-but-very-disappointed voice of his, as if I am three years old – not twelve years, twenty-one weeks and one day!

3. Nolly would understand but wouldn't want Mum upset. She'd say something like, *Leave things be, lass.* OR *Don't upset the applecart.*

4. What if I did find him but he didn't want to know me?

5. What if he's horrible?

So, the result is:

FOR trying to trace my dad, **eight** points

FOR NOT trying to trace my dad, **five** points only.

The winner is...

FOR trying to trace my dad...

That's scary. But **I DESPERATELY NEED TO KNOW WHO MY DAD IS!** What am I going to do? And how am I going to do it?

Monday, 29th November

7.10. Mum and Ian get back from their honeymoon this evening.

16.40. Back from school. No one at home. Called upstairs for Nolly – then remembered.

She doesn't live here any more! Ever since I was little, Nolly was always there in her upstairs flat when I needed her.

16.50. Found a note from Aunt B. She has gone walkies with Buster. I went up to Nolly's anyway. All her furniture's still here but without Nolly it's a ghost town. No Virgin Mary standing on the mantelpiece. No cup of tea and ginger nuts to greet me after school. No beige anorak on the hook. No photos of me on the sideboard. No baby me in my bouncer. No infant school nativity play – me as the donkey. And there won't be £1.50 for painting her toenails or pocket money for all other little jobs I did for her. **No Nolly!** Boo-hoo.

Aunt Beryl is using Nolly's old bedroom. I had a little sneak. **She wears Snoopy jim-jams!** And she's reading a book called *Twenty-one of the World's Most Cunning Criminals.* Also, she has a secret stash of cough candy and rum truffles.

Found Graemella and Twinkle kissing through the wire of their runs. Think they have made friends! Will try putting them in together for a little while each day to see how they get on.

20.35. **Mum and Ian are home!** Ian carried

Mum across the threshold – sort of. Mum must be getting very heavy with that huge tum and three babies because Ian was going quite red in the face and Aunt Beryl had to give him a hand. Mum and Ian looked a bit gobsmacked to see the furniture covered with kitchen foil.

My first night at home with my stepfather. Mum is Mrs Deborah Tanner now. I am still Finch **Penny** though. Aunt B. leaves tomorrow. Ian's taking her to the airport in the morning. She has left a wedding parcel for Bill and Nolly. It is **very** heavy. She says if we have any trouble from Buster we can open it as we will find it very useful. Mum says she hopes it's a ball and chain, which is stupid because it is rectangular not spherical. Made her a cup of tea. Mum's bosoms are truly **ENORMOUS**. She looks like a cross between Miss Piggy and a Teletubby.

Tuesday, 30th November

7.45. I helped Mum take all the foil off the furniture.

17.40. Went to Jay's after school. He gave me a packet of LOVEHEARTS and we took turns to pick. His first one to me said TRUE LOVE. Mine to him said, MY BOY

His to me: GREAT LIPS!

Mine to him:

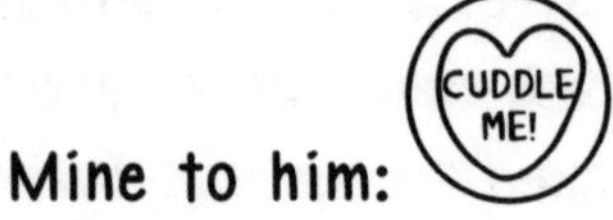

So he did! And he smelt of soap and chewing gum and it was delicious. Then we had a liquorice shoelace race, nibbling from each end till we met up in the middle with a sticky kiss. I felt all tingly and melty and weird. **Is this what S.E.X. is like?** It's sort of scary, but nice too. My tongue is all black.

Afterwards, I explained to him how, since my mum told me the truth about my real dad, I haven't been able to stop thinking about him. Every day he pops into my head, just the way she described him, tall and slim, with dark hair. And my biggest wish is to find him.

He said, *What does your mum say about that?*

I said, *Don't be stupid! I can't tell her! It would make her feel bad about all those lies she told me and it would remind her of the horrible times with her aunt and uncle, and running away, and finding herself pregnant and all alone. If I'm going to try to find my dad, I'd have to do it secretly.*

He said, *You're not serious?* I told him how serious I was. He said, *You must be crazy then!*

I said, *Trust me. I have thought this through very carefully, and I'm a bit disappointed that you don't understand. This is REALLY IMPORTANT to me! How would you feel if you were in my place?*

He said, *I'd think it through more and I'd talk it over with my mum too.*

I sighed, *But I just told you! I don't want to upset my mum! For starters, I'm not even sure that it's possible to find him. And I'm not going to risk upsetting her for nothing. It's better my way. If I do manage to trace him, then of course I'd tell her!* I told him that I was rather hoping he'd help me. But if he was going to be so difficult, I'd have to manage without him.

I said, ***I have made up my mind to look for him! And I'm not giving up now!***

He said, ***OK! OK!*** *But how exactly are you going to do that?*

I said, *I don't know yet. But I'll find out!*

Then he said, *All I'm saying is maybe you should think about it a bit more.*

I told him, *Look, I never* **stop** *thinking about it!*

He said, *I know! That's the problem. It's become an obsession. The other problem is you've got this picture in your head of some sort of wonderful fantasy dad. What if he's not like that? What if you don't like him? You might never be able to get rid of him. What if he's like Mr Sowerbutts?* (And actually that is a very scary thought. Mr Sowerbutts, also known as **Mr Sourbreath**, is our Geography teacher. He has very bad dandruff too and is **always** in a bad mood.) I'm all mixed up now. Why did Jay have to mention Mr Sowerbutts? I can't get him out of my head!

16.10. Found Graemella sniffing Twinkle in a friendly sort of way. Twinkle sniffed her back. It looked like they were kissing! I wanted to cuddle them up but didn't want to interrupt, so I just watched. I think they've made friends!

17.40. Mum and Ian have gone shopping. Phoned Kerry about my idea of searching for my dad and my tiff with Jay over it. She already knew! Jay had told Dan and Dan then told Kerry. Unlike me they are living in the 21st century and have mobile phones. She thinks that Jay can be a bit of a fuddy-duddy sometimes, which is probably true because his parents are quite old. Kerry is very excited about the idea of trying to find my dad though. Thanks Kerry! Also told her about the Lovehearts and liquorice kissing with Jay. She's going to get some Lovehearts and liquorice for Dan.

19.05. If anyone is obsessed, it's Ian. He's obsessed with babies! He came home with a huge pile of books from the library about childbirth. Had to endure him reading out

INTERESTING FACTS

during dinner. E.g. The placenta is the baby's life-support system. This is attached from the mother's uterus to the baby by the umbilical cord. Twins and triplets can be formed when a single egg splits. **PER-LEEZ!** Not when I'm eating my omelette!

20.15. Phoned Cassie about the kissing. We are meeting up after school tomorrow at the **Ice Cream-Dream Machine**. Told her I'm skint. She said, *Don't worry, lovey.* Lovey must be her new word. I think I might have to pinch it.

20.20. Ian has just had a go at me for 'monopolising' the phone because he is waiting for an **important** phone call from a client wanting a quote for painting the house. Told him, *Look, lovey, if I had a mobile like all my mates, I wouldn't need to monopolise the phone, would I?!*

21.15. A miracle has happened! Buster has not sat on the furniture! He sits in his dog bed! Guarding it!

21.35. In bed. I have stuck the photo of my make-believe dad at the end of my bed, and I am staring at it to wipe out the image of Mr Sowerbutts that keeps popping into my head. It's not working yet. **It's all Jay's fault!**

Wednesday, 1st December

7.10. Woken up by Buster licking my face.

YEE-**UK!** It's Ian's fault. He's too soft with him. He thinks it's mean to shut him in the kitchen! Aunt B. will be very cross. All that training down the drain! Had nightmare about Mr Sowerbutts. It was a geography lesson and I was calling him Daddy!

***16.45.* The weirdest thing!** At lunchtime, we were on rota duty in the W.Y.P? helpline office. This message had been sent in!!

I need some advice. My mum had me when she was 16. My dad doesn't know anything about me because she moved away before she knew she was pregnant. She doesn't like talking about him much and says it's all in the past. I have a stepdad now and he's OK. My nan told me that I look just like my dad. I think about him all the time. I don't think it would be too hard to find him. I'd really like to let him know about me, but I know my mum would go bonkers about him. What can I do?
Desperately Seeking Father, Year Eight.

It was so SPOOKY! I wanted to shout, *That's just like me!* But there was no way I was going to let bossy Angela and Snooty Sophie

(Year Tens) earwig my life story. They must have thought something weird was going on, 'cos Kerry was nudging me and waggling her eyebrows, like she was saying, *Hey! That's not you, is it?* Jay and Dan were giving me funny looks too.

Here are some of the answers that came in:

• I think you should talk it over with your mother first. If she's not happy about it, then don't do it. You could hurt her very very much.

N.K. Year Nine

• Don't even think about it! Are you mad? Wait until you're eighteen when you are adult enough to make big decisions and take the consequences.

Snoopy, Year Ten

• If it was me, I'd really want to know who my dad was. If he didn't want to know I'd be upset, but at least I'd have tried. It would be difficult if I didn't like him though.

S.P and M.Y. Year Nine

• I just had to write in. You sound just like me, except I know where my dad lives but my mum won't let me have anything to do with him.

I don't think this is fair, neither does my nan. Me and Mum have lots of rows about it. I think adults can be wrong and selfish sometimes. Mum divorced my dad, but I didn't.

GIRL, Year Nine

• It would be a big shock when your dad finds out about you. He might be mad with your mum for not telling him about you. Also I think your mum would be mad about you being sneaky behind her back.

Girl, Year Eight

• What if your dad doesn't want to know you? Could you take it? It would be very upsetting. I'd wait till I was older if I were you.

Elvis, Year Ten

• This happened to me. My parents split up when I was a baby and my dad brought me up. I didn't think about her much till I was eleven and started asking my dad about her. He found out where she was living and we met up. I didn't like her very much but I'm glad I met her. It makes me appreciate what a good dad I've got.

J.J. Year Ten

• Your mum should be more understanding about your feelings. I would want to know.

Craig, Year Eight

• You are being selfish. Your mum would be very hurt and never trust you again. Let it go until you're old enough to handle it.

Three girls, Year Nine

• Your mum is the one who has cared for you. How can you even think about doing this behind her back? You are making a BIG MISTAKE and being so selfish! She might never forgive you or trust you again. Talk to her about it first.

Steve

• What if there's a good reason why your mum doesn't want to talk about him? What if she's trying to protect you from the truth? What if he's not a nice person? Think about it.

K.&S. Year Eight

• This is a tough one, isn't it? There is no simple solution. Would you like to have a chat about it? You could come and see me any lunchtime or after school. Put a note in my pigeonhole, or e-mail me at ms.moody@fletchleyhigh.sch.uk

Sophie was twittering on with, *How perfectly sad! Let's hope he sees sense, poor child.* I wanted to strangle her with her long perfectly highlighted hair. Jay was looking at me with a big smug look as if to say, *Hey! That's just like you! And see what everyone is saying? They're saying what I think. It's a dumb idea.*

As soon as we left the office, Jay said, *Well, that was interesting. Hey, it wasn't you, was it, who posted that question about searching for a father?*

I told him, *I don't need to ask for advice, thanks. Like I told you, I've made up my mind.* He said, *Did you notice that it was seven to three against?*

Dan just stood there, saying nothing and keeping a low profile as usual, so I asked him what **he** thought about me trying to find my dad. He shrugged, *Don't ask me.* Which is a typical Dan-type answer.

Kerry said, *Don't worry, Finch. I'm on your side, whatever, right?*

Then Jay looked at me and said, *But that's not the point, is it? The point is that it could have been you. And like me, some kids think that trying to find a lost father without telling their mother is a dumb idea.*

I told him, *Of course I'd tell my mum! But not until I'd found him!*

Jay said, *And why would you do that?*

I said, ***You know why!*** *Because, she'd probably try to stop me! But...* He didn't let me finish, just nodded, *Exactly!* And he walked off! Dan went with him.

16.55. Why haven't you called me, Jay? Call me and apologise so that I can forgive you and we can make up. I need you to help me!

17.15. Ian is **dead mad** with Buster. He buried himself in the compost heap (Buster, not Ian). Then he came charging into the kitchen covered in smelly, slimy leaves and grass cuttings and the stinky straw full of poos from Graemella's and Twinkle's hutch. Mum tried to shove him out with the mop but he thought it was a game of tug-of-war and was dragging Mum round the room till Ian rescued her.

He's locked him in the shed. I can hear him howling. Mum is lying down. Little Twinkle was **very frightened** and hid behind Graemella who thumped her feet and **screamed** at Buster. Buster yelped and ran off. **What a coward!** If Graemella were human she'd be very bossy and scary and say things like *Who are you looking at?* and *Get lost!* And she'd pinch your crisps at break time. She'd get loads of detentions for answering back and go round with a gang of boys or rough girls. But she would be funny too and stick up for her mates if they were in trouble. She'd be very bright but would hate school. Twinkle would chatter and giggle in class a lot. She would be very popular with the boys because of her prettiness and girly, funny ways and her giggling. Some girls would find her **very** annoying.

17.30. I wrote that to take my mind off JAY. But he's popped back in again. **Why hasn't he called me?**

18.20. Ian and I have decided to open Aunt B.'s present to Bill and Nolly. Ian says he hopes it's a stun gun.

18.30 It is not a stun gun. It is two things. One is a voucher for six weeks of dog training classes for Bill and Buster. The other is a book called **TRAINING YOUR DOG THE KIRKALDY WAY**, by Beryl Kirkaldy (Aunt Beryl).

18.40. Still no apology from Jay!

18.45. Ian has found my trainer in the compost heap. It is stinky and slimy and full of worms. I told him that I am taking charge of Buster's training until Nolly and Bill get back on Monday. He was very pleased and says he will buy me a new pair of trainers. I also told him that I need to have a **serious** talk with Mum and him about pocket money. I am cooking dinner tonight. Frozen pizza and chips. I know this is not very healthy but it's all that we've got except for eggs, and I'm not risking eggs again in case Ian starts on about placentas and stuff.

19.10. Had a Buster-free dinner, apart from his howling and scratching at the window. Ian has taken him walkies.

JAY! CALL ME! NOW!

19.20. Buster has arrived home alone.

19.28. Ian just arrived home. He is in a terrible mood and called Buster lots of **very rude** names.

21.35. **Jay! Why haven't you called me!** You're only making me **even more mad** with you!

Thursday, 2nd December

17.50. Loads of news!

1. Jay sent me this note in Geography.

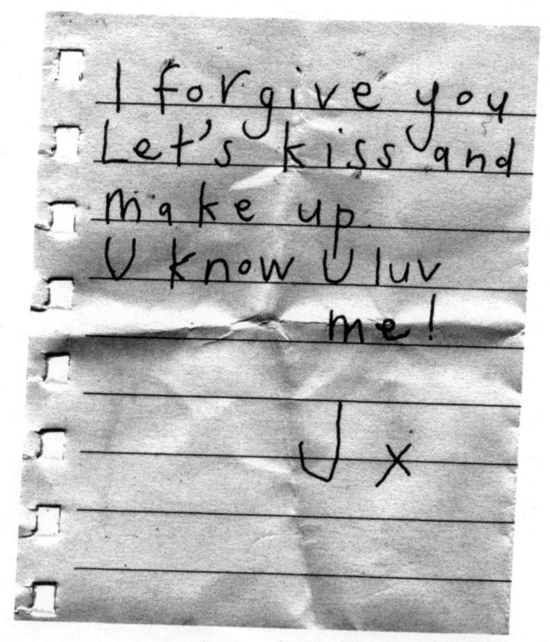
I forgive you
Let's kiss and
make up.
U know U luv
me!

J x

I sent a note back saying, *Sorry, but I cannot forgive YOU! I need you to help me, but you won't. You are forcing me to choose between you and my father! How can you do this to me?*
2. Met up with Cassie at **The Ice Cream-Dream Machine** after school. Had one scoop each of chocolate cherry, mango and passion fruit and coconut raisin. It was so YUMMY that I nearly fainted. **It cost £3.90!** Cassie told me she gets **£25 pocket money a week!** For doing NOTHING! £10 from her mum and £15 from her dad. The divorce is costing him loads of money. Cassie will be moving soon. Since the divorce her dad has moved into a flat with his girlfriend. Cassie's mum is buying a smaller house. I told Cass all about my mission to find my dad. She got very excited and said, *You* ***have*** *to do it! Now that you've started thinking about it, it won't ever go away. It will be like a little worm nibbling away inside your brain!*

I said, *I know! That's exactly what it feels like! I thought Jay would want to help me, but he won't! So I'm going to have to do it on my own, somehow. He's being totally boring and bossy and saying I should talk it over with Mum first! I wish I'd never told*

him now! I already know that Mum wouldn't want me trying to find him. But if I did find him, of course I would tell her! And then she'd realise how much it means to me, and she might change her mind. And maybe I could write to him and we could meet up.
Cass said, *Wow! This is really important to you, isn't it? But there's an awful lot of IFs and MAYBEs. I wish I could help, lovey! I'll think about it!*

20.20. I'm trying to take my mind off things by reading Aunt B.'s book about dog training. It is mega interesting. I shall insist with Ian that we follow these rules:
1. Buster to be put out while we eat our breakfast, or into another room if it is bad weather, until he can behave himself and learn not to snatch food from us.
2. Ian and I will take turns to sit in Buster's dog bed to teach him that we are the TOP DOGS.
3. We must ignore Buster if he tries to get attention by nudging and pawing and **ONLY REWARD HIM** WHEN HE IS **GOOD!**

I have put Ian in charge of teaching Buster to

SIT, STAND, STAY and **NOT TO JUMP UP** and given him the book to read. (Pages 98 to 132.) I asked him about pocket money too. He said he thought **£5 a week** was reasonable. I laughed hilariously. Told him I will do a pocket money survey of my mates, and I'll let him know the going rate.

22.05. **Jay, oh Jay!** How can you be so cruel? **I need you!** You should have apologised by now!

Only twenty-three days to Christmas! No one will be getting presents from me unless my pocket money crisis is sorted.

19.30. Mum has gone to bed. She is very tired. I'm a bit worried about her. So is Ian. **I have so many worries!**

Friday, 3rd December

7.40. According to Ian's homemade pregnancy chart on the kitchen wall, Mum is eighteen weeks pregnant and she should be feeling the babies kicking by now. Mum says it feels more like a herd of **elephants**. Tried to get a word in about my pocket money crisis but Ian has babies on the brain and was waffling on to Mum about eating up the prunes he'd bought to help with her constipation problem. She **hates** prunes. Desperately need some money to buy a present for Sabine's thirteenth birthday sleepover tomorrow.

16.25

Pocket money survey

Here are the results so far.
KERRY gets **£5 basic a week.** She earns extra for emptying the dishwasher (***50p* a time**), emptying all the bins (***£1***), and taking her mum and dad a cup of tea in bed on Sunday mornings (***£1.50***). But she's thinking of stopping that 'cos she'd rather have a lie-in. They don't care if her room is messy. The most she's earned was ***£15*** but the **average per week** = ***£10***. She buys most of her own clothes.
SARA gets ***£10* a week.** She buys her own mags and some of her clothes. She has to empty the dishwasher every day. She cleans her own room 'cos she doesn't like her mum going in there. She earns extra from doing the ironing.
SABINE picks up her little sister from school every day and looks after her till her mum

gets home from work. She helps with shopping and housework. (Her mum and dad are separated.) She's supposed to get **£5 each** from her mum and dad, though her dad isn't very reliable and she doesn't always get it. She sometimes earns extra from her nan for doing shopping. She saves up to buy clothes, but her mum buys some of them. This all comes to anything between **£5 to £10 a week** plus **£3 a week** for gymnastics club, which her mum pays for.
MIA gets **£15 a week!** Plus ballet lessons. She goes shopping with her mum who buys her anything she likes, also all her mags. She doesn't have to do any jobs!
NARINDER gets **£10 a week** from her dad and her grandad usually gives her **£5**. She also has piano lessons. She earns extra by doing the ironing and looking after the goldfish. She puts most of it into her bank account. **She has saved £202!** Her mum pays for most of her clothes, but she buys her own too.
DAN gets **£10 pocket money** plus **£5 clothing allowance**, so buys his own clothes. His parents pay for his Fletchley United season ticket. He has to feed the rabbits and guinea pigs and clean out the cages. Hard

work! **NOT!** I cannot believe that he gets ***£60* a month** just for that! He saves most of it so that he can buy a car when he's seventeen!
JAY. I'm not talking to Jay until he apologises.
ME. I keep my room tidy – unlike Mum!
I look after Twinkle and Graemella and clean their hutch. I ***AM*** the **DISHWASHER!!** Also the **DOG-TRAINER!** I help with the vacuum cleaning and the dusting. Since Nolly left, what do I get? **ZILCH!**
I am SHOCKED! I never realised how poor I am. Something must be done about it.

Dear Mum and Ian,
It has come to my notice that I am down to 9p. This is because I don't get any regular pocket money since Nolly moved out. I have done a pocket money survey, (attached). All my friends get pocket money and some don't even do any jobs. I have drawn up a chart of jobs and fees.
Washing up
50p X 2 every day = £1 a day
x 7 = **£7 a week**
Vacuum cleaning once a week
= **£5**

Making my bed and **keeping room tidy**

At 50p a day x 7 = **£3.50 a week**

Also, **training Buster to behave**,

50p a day x 7 = **£3.50 a week**

(I will not charge for looking after Twinkle and Graemella because they are my responsibility.)

TOTAL IS ***£19* a week!**

I am willing to negotiate terms. I need to sort this urgently as I have to buy a present for Sabine's birthday.

I will have to pick the right moment to give this to them to discuss it. I think I should get some back pay.

Saturday, 4th December

Warrior Princess Sleepover at Sabine's tonight!

9.10. Ian has taken Mum to the doctors because she is not feeling well. This is probably *not* a good time to ask about pocket money.

10.15. I am writing this in Buster's dog bed. He keeps looking at me with a sad face but he's stopped that annoying whimpering. Have done two loads of washing, Hoovered and dusted. Feel like Cinderella. **Why hasn't**

Jay called me? Have we broken up? I'm feeling **depressed**.

10.55. Mum is home. The doctor says she has high blood pressure and MUST STOP WORK and **REST**. She is lying on the sofa. I made her a cup of tea. Showed Ian my pocket money survey. He said, *Blimey. Is this what kids get these days? Are you joking me?* He gave me a fiver to get a present for Sabine, but the meany wants a receipt and the change back. Told him that I urgently need to discuss my pocket-money crisis. He says he'll talk it over with Mum when she's feeling a bit better. **Weeh-hee!** Asked him how he was getting on with training Buster to obey orders. He saluted and clicked his heels and said, *Yes, ma'am! Starting today, ma'am!* Ha-ha.

15.55. Bought Sabine a daisy necklace for £2.99.

Sunday, 5th December

***11.05.* AWESOME sleepover at Sabine's!** Not that we did much sleeping! Kerry started on about how COOL Dan is and that his kisses turn her legs to jelly! Narinder said, *You'd better watch out! Don't get carried away! You don't want to get pregnant!* We exploded into shrieks of laughter.

Kerry screamed, *Narinder! I said kisses! You can't get pregnant from kissing!*

Narinder said, *I know that! But I'm not joking! My mum's a doctor at the Family Planning Clinic and you wouldn't believe how many twelve and thirteen-year-old girls turn up pregnant. They start with kissing, then they get carried away and don't know when to stop. Or rather, the boy doesn't!*

Kerry snorted, *Don't worry! I know where to stop, thanks!*

I said, *Me too. Kisses and cuddles,* ***FULL STOP!***

Mia said, *Oh, don't take any notice of Narinder! What does she know? She's never even* ***had*** *a boyfriend!* Narinder started to say something, but Mia barged in with, *As it happens, I have a new boyfriend! He's fourteen. He lives two doors away and* *he's in Year Nine.* We all went, ***Oooooo!***

Kerry said, *Can you imagine having a baby at our age! I don't want babies till I'm forty! I want to live it up first!*

Then Narinder said, *My mum told me that I was conceived on a beach in the Seychelles. It was very romantic.*

Sabine said, *Wow! That is* ***so*** *beautiful!*

Kerry said, *I think I'd throw up if my mum told me where I was conceived! I don't want to know, thanks!*

I said, *I know where I was conceived – at a party, but all I know about my dad is that his name was Tom, he was tall, had dark hair, and I look like him. I think about him all the time.*

Sara asked, *Hey! Was it you who sent that message to the school website, then?*

I said, *No. But it sounded just like me. I'd really like to find my dad.*

Our warrior princess costumes are getting very tatty. All my gold stars have fallen off my skirt and it's covered in chocolate splodges. I think we need to reinvent ourselves. Sara thinks we should be more feminine.

12.10. Kerry phoned for a gossip about Mia. She says she doesn't know why Narinder puts up with the way Mia puts her down and bosses her about. We have formed the Stick-up-for-Narinder-Party.

14.10. Just rushed to the phone hoping it was Jay calling to apologise. But it was Cassie, saying, *Get over here! NOW!* ***QUICK!*** *Before my mum gets back!*

17.20. Cassie is a **true friend. What would I do without her?** Their house was full of packing boxes because they're moving next week. She said, *Listen, I want to show you something.* She led me into her mum's bedroom where her mum's computer was. She said, *First you have to swear that you won't tell my mum. She'd go loopy if she knew I'd been snooping.* So I promised, and then Cassie said, *Have you heard of a website called FRIENDS REUNITED?*

I said, *Yeah, it's where people search for their old school friends or something.*

She said, *Right. And my mum has become totally* ***addicted*** *to it!!*

There, on the screen were all these

messages from her mum's old school friends, loads of photos too. Old class photos of teenagers in school uniform, and in football kit, and netball teams, and photos of them now, grown up, some with their families and cars. She pointed to a boy in the second row of one of the class photos. He had sticky-out ears and a long nose. She said, *That was Mum's **boyfriend** when she was sixteen.*
We laughed so much, we had to lie down. She snorted, *It's not really funny! They're planning to meet up! What if she likes him and they get together? But that's not really the point! Don't you see what I'm getting at?*

I joked, *Well, your dad has sticky-out ears too so perhaps that's the sort of men she goes for!*

She said, ***NO**, STUPID! The point is that this could be a way of **finding out more about your dad!** All you have to do is join Friends Reunited – and **pretend to be your mum!** There must be loads of people who were at that party where she met your dad Tom. Maybe people who know what he's doing and where he is!*
It was as if a **bright light** had switched on

inside my head. Why hadn't I thought of that? She showed me how the website worked. Since then I haven't been able to think about anything else! **Cassie, I owe you a million favours!**

............Action Plan............

1. I'll tell Mum that we're doing a school project comparing education and schools now, with those of our parents. A crafty idea I think!
2. Quiz Mum about her school days, her old friends – names and stories and teachers and stuff so that I can make out that I'm Mum when I get chatting to her old friends.
3. Find £7.50 to join *Friends Reunited* and find someone who will loan me their credit card.
4. Chat to Mum's old mates and ask if anyone remembers **Tom**, the boy she got pregnant by! **MY DAD!**
5. Find out all I can about him.
6. And then... **Oh help! This is getting scary.**

Should I be doing this? Mum would go **crazy** if she knew what I was doing!

18.20. Kerry phoned. She says that Dan has told her something about Jay that I would be really mad about if I knew! I said, *Tell me! Tell me!* But she has been sworn to secrecy! This is **agony! Everything is happening at once!**

Monday, 6th December

16.25. **I know! I know Dan's secret about Jay!** Kerry didn't tell me exactly. She acted it out, which we decided does not count as telling. First she flapped her arms like wings and pointed at me. I said, *Is it a bird?* She nodded and made a 'sort of ' expression, and pointed at me again. I said, *Is it **about** me?* She nodded again. Then she repeated the flapping wings again. I said, *Another bird?* She nodded madly. I asked, *Do you mean **Jay?*** She nodded so hard I thought her head would come off. She pretended to be typing something.

I asked, *Someone writing a letter?* She nodded and started to write something in the air. **W.Y.P?** I burst **What's your problem?** *Something to do with the W.Y.P? website? Someone writing to the website?* She nodded. I said, *But I haven't written anything to the website.* She sighed, *I know! So who does that leave?* I said, *Jay?* She screamed, **Yes!** I thought for a bit, and gasped, *Are you trying to say that Jay wrote to the W.Y.P? website?* She nodded furiously. **What did he write??** She acted out pages and pages of writing. Then I got it. I said, *Is this anything to do with that message from* **Desperately Seeking Father?** She burst, *Not only did Jay write that message – he wrote some of the replies too!* ***But only the ones saying what a dumb idea it is!*** *I don't know how many, but some of them were FAKE! He thought it might make you change your mind about looking for your dad! You know how much he's always saying it's a bad idea.*

I AM SO MAD WITH JAY!

Just wait till I see him! I'm not talking to him. I have written a letter.

Jay, I cannot call you **'Dear'** Jay as I am **deeply** hurt. It has come to my notice that you faked that message to W.Y.P? about searching for a lost father, and **ALSO some of the replies!** If you thought that you could make me give up the search **you are mistaken!** In fact I am **even more determined!** So there! I really trusted you, you know! **How could you do this to me?**
Your ex-girlfriend,

Finch

17.20. Pedalled round to Jay's and posted the letter through his letterbox.

17.35. Jay phoned. I refused to talk to him. Mum says I'm being mean to him. What would she say if she knew what it was all about? **DON'T THINK ABOUT IT!**

17.45. Kerry phoned. Dan just phoned her. He's mad with her for telling me about Jay's fake message.

18.00. **Jay, Jay! Why are you doing this to me?**

18.25. Ian and Buster have just given Mum and me a dog obedience demonstration. Buster can now **SIT** and **STAY** to order! Gave them both a pat on the head.
19.55. Managed to make a quick call on the kitchen phone to Dan, while Mum and Ian were watching telly. Told him not to be mad with Kerry because I had guessed that Jay had sent those messages. Also she is my best friend and best friends shouldn't be expected to lie to each other!

Haven't had a second to quiz Mum about her school days.

Tuesday, 7th December

16.05. No one home. And someone has been in my room! The carpet is rolled back and the creaky floorboard is up. I nearly used it for hiding my diary! There is a note on the kitchen table which says,

[illegible] with Buster.

Fortunately I can read Mum's handwriting.

She and Buster are at Nolly and Bill's flat. I have to go.

20.50. **Loads of news.**

Mum's scan showed that she has **definitely** got **three** little babies in her tum! They are much clearer on the new scan. They are all developing very nicely. They can't be definite about what sex they are yet 'cos they were all curled up. They could hear **three** lots of tiny heartbeats! Aaah.

Nolly and Bill have gone **orange**. I'm not sure that sunbathing is good for old people. They showed us their holiday snaps that they took with their new digital camera. Most of them were of Nolly in her bikini. She brought back some fake designer sunglasses for

me. They are COOL. Ian joined us there after work and we had take-away fish and chips. Bill gave me some castanets. Ian and Buster did a demonstration of **SIT**, **STAND** and **STAY**. Nolly was very impressed, even though

Buster sat on her Spanish sun hat. Ian says he wants a dog. Mum says **NO WAY**. Nolly has already signed Bill up for dog obedience classes.

I'm still not talking to Jay. Narinder went round with me, Kerry, Sara and Sabine at breaks today because Mia went off with her boyfriend. Jay was away from school today. Dan says he's got a painful toe and can't walk. He got it from trying to kick a brick. Dan is mad that I know about Jay sending those fake messages and doesn't believe that Kerry didn't tell me. And apparently Jay is mad with Dan for telling Kerry in the first place. I'm still mad with Jay. The **mystery** of my bedroom floor is solved. Ian has taken up the floorboard to check where the water pipes run because he's going to turn the two flats back to a proper house before the triplet-babes arrive. There will be four bedrooms upstairs, an en suite for Mum and Ian, and a bathroom. Downstairs there will be a kitchen-diner, a sitting room, a shower and utility room and an office for Ian. Instead of a small flat we will have **A PROPER HOUSE!!** I have chosen the L-shaped bedroom with the slopey roof. I **ADORE** it!

Wednesday, 8th December

15.55. Jay still away. Dan says he's broken his big toe. Kerry said she thinks that in one way, it's kind of cute that Jay went to all that trouble with the faked messages and that he must really care about me even if he was out of order.

16.10. **Jay phoned me!** He says he's really sorry about upsetting me and only did it because he doesn't want me getting hurt or taking risks. He says he's been missing me like **mad!**

17.25. I have been to see Jay. We have kissed and made up. I think the problem is we are both a bit bossy and we both think we're right. I'm bossy in a **noisy** sort of way. Jay is bossy in a quiet, secretive sort of way. Not **all** the messages were fake. Just the one from *Desperately Seeking Father, Year Eight*, and the reply from *Elvis, Year Ten*. I took him some Lovehearts. They said, YOU ARE MINE, BE TRUE, TRUST ME and BAD BOY

I know that he **really, really** means what he says because he's agreed to help with my search for my dad! And I agreed that if we do find him, I'll tell Mum and not make any contact without her permission. And I'm happy with that. Sometimes my ideas grow so **big** the sensible bit of me gets squashed flat. I'll need to sound convincingly like Mum when I get chatting on-line to her old school mates, so I'd better start quizzing her about her schooldays straight away.

21.20. In bed. Ian was out this evening so got Mum talking about school. Once she got going I couldn't stop her! Got **loads** of names of her friends and teachers. I am keeping a secret file.

☆ Her best friend was a girl called **Dawn Cooper.**

☆ And a **MEGA CLUE!** It was AT DAWN'S SIXTEENTH birthday party that Mum met my dad Tom and got pregnant with me.

☆ Dawn and Mum used to play in the netball team together.

☆ Dawn was mad about a boy called Steve Todd who all the girls fancied.

☆ Mum and Dawn went round with two other girls called Daniella and Denise.

☆ They were known as the four **Ds**.

☆ Her favourite subjects were English, P.E. and Games. (I **hate** P.E. and Games!) I got loads of stuff about teachers too.

☆ She says she often thinks of them and wonders what they're doing!

I asked her why she didn't keep in touch with her mates. I said, *You could've written, or phoned – I bet they were really worried about you!* She said she'd wished lots of times that she had, but she was too terrified that her uncle might find out where she was and come looking for her and make her go back. He used to beat her for the **slightest** thing, like what she was wearing, or how she looked at him, or wearing make-up or eating food without permission. Sometimes she didn't even know what she'd done wrong. She had tried to phone Dawn once, just to let her know she was OK. But then she panicked that he'd somehow trace her so she slammed the phone down quickly.

This is what else I found out.

☆ The name of her school was Queen Elizabeth High School, Swindon, known as Q.E. School for short.

☆ She missed doing all her G.C.S.Es when she ran away.

21.50. Mum has been sitting on my bed for half an hour telling me more stories about her schoolmates and teachers and stuff. I am exhausted. Got to write it all down in my file. It's going to be a cinch pretending to be Mum. I wonder if her uncle and aunt are still alive and living in the same house? They sound so cruel and mean. I'd like to tell them what I think of them!

Thursday, 9th December

Only sixteen days to **Christmas!**

17.40. Jay is back at school. He's got crutches. We held hands under the table in Geography. Had to colour in the British coastline with my left hand which was very tricky and I accidentally coloured part of Wales blue too so it disappeared into the Irish Sea. Fusspot-Sowerbutts is making me do it again for homework. Donna Siddley was a pain in Games today, snatching towels and chortling at girls with small boobs. Just because hers are like **melons!** Kerry got her own back and snatched Donna's towel. She is

SO HAIRY! **Everywhere!** I shall never complain again about my wispy bits! Better than looking like **Ape Girl**. Sally Russell is totally hairless. Which is weird 'cos her periods started when she was eleven. I'll need to ask Mum for a razor for my underarms soon. I offered Paula Scott a squirt of my anti-perspirant. She sweats a lot and can be really pongy sometimes. She made a snooty face and said, *My family don't believe in using artificial chemicals!* I feel sorry for her. And for anyone who has to sit next to her. Her mum should be reported for cruelty to children. It's cruel to Paula and us!

19.05. Pocket money sorted! **£10 a week!**
I can't believe it!
JOBS
Keep my room clean and tidy – which is a bit much coming from Mum who has some very messy habits.
Wash or wipe up daily.
Vacuum cleaning once a week.
Clean out cages for Twinkle and Graemella.
Pay for my own mags and beauty stuff.
Mum and Ian will pay for my shoes.

I can earn more from extra jobs and buy some of my own clothes! I am **rich!**

Friday, 10th December

7.45. Our house is full of Ian's mates moving furniture and bashing walls down. In my new room there's an old chest of drawers, which has a lock and key! **At last!** Somewhere to keep my diary! I will wear the key on a chain round my neck to keep it safe. I'll be glad when the wallpaper goes. It's orange and green stripes. It makes me go cross-eyed. Plenty of room for sleepovers though.

17.35. Went round to Jay's with Dan and Kerry after school. Kerry's hair has started to grow. She looks like a criminal. She's collected a total of £118.73 in sponsor money from the Shave Rave and the Wear-a-hat-or-wig day! I only managed £21.05. But the total raised for a new scanner is...**£2,498.65!**

Saturday 11th December

16.40. Mum and me went to Nolly's to escape the noise and mess. Bill and Buster had gone for a bike ride. Nolly is planning to buy her own computer. She says Bill spends so much time on his that she feels like a computer widow. She wants me to teach her how to use it. Gave her an hour's lesson on Bill's computer. She will pay me **£5 an hour!** I am **mega-rich!** Went Christmas shopping this afternoon with Kerry.

For Ian, deodorising shoe insoles, £2.49
For Mum, a triple-frame photo-stand for the triplets, £4.99
For Nolly, a Sean Connery mouse mat, £3.50
For Bill, a nostril-hair trimmer, £2.29

My horoscope today says that this week I will comfort a friend and make progress on a search for information! Also someone may put me under pressure over a personal matter. I was born under the water sign of Cancer, the crab. I can be **tough** on the outside, but soft on the inside. My bad points are that I can be stubborn. But I am in good company, because the Princess of Wales was a Cancer sign and so is the Dalai Lama. Like them I am quite wise and sensible. I am also inclined to be romantic and dreamy. I have a good memory. Unfortunately I am a worrier, but I have excellent intuition.

Sunday, 12th December

17.05. Asked Mum if I can have a sleepover in my new room on Saturday. She said **YES!** My intuition was correct!

19.15. Everyone is coming to my sleepover – Kerry, Narinder, Mia, Sabine, and Sara.

20.10. In my room, trying to escape from Ian reading aloud from his new *Encyclopaedia of Pregnancy, Childbirth and Childcare.* He says that the babies' eyes will be opening about now (nineteen weeks), but they can't see properly yet. I'm not surprised. It must be very dark in there. They'd need headlamps to see anything!

21.25. In bed.
Have had a **STUNNING IDEA** for my sleepover. Instead of warrior princesses, we will be...**THE ZODIAC GIRLS!** And I've invented a game called, **GUESS WHOSE STAR SIGN THIS IS.**

Before the sleepover I'll get everyone to

write their star sign onto a piece of paper, fold it up small and put them all into a bag. Then we take it in turns to pick one out and research the characteristics of that star sign. At the sleepover we'll take turns to read them out and guess whose star sign it is! A brilliant game I think! Invented by yours truly. I've been so busy I haven't had time to worry about Mum and looking for my dad. But now I've started worrying again.

Monday, 13th December

17.40. Learned a French carol in music today. I can't stop singing it. The triplets could be born bilingual! Made a pop-up Christmas card in C.D.T. It's a boy and girl's head under a sprig of mistletoe. When you open and close the card, their heads move as if they are kissing. It's for Jay. It was very hard to stop him seeing it. Had to move to another table but he kept coming over.

Tuesday, 14th December

Had drama today. Miss Lamb told us the story of *The Sugar Plum Fairy*, how the nutcracker and other presents under the Christmas tree came to life. We had to get into groups and make up our own stories to the music. The best group would get Friday morning off school to perform their piece at the infants' school assembly.

Our group was me, Jay, Kerry, Dan, Narinder and Mia, Sabine and Sara, but we were forced to have Shane and his mate Neil in our group. We made up a brilliant story of a giant Christmas cracker that two children find at midnight. When they pull it, all the toys inside come to life. I was a floppy rag doll, Kerry was a clown, Jay was a clockwork soldier, Dan was Thomas the tank engine, Mia was a fairy, Narinder was a jack in the box and Sara and Sabine were the two children. Unfortunately Shane and Neil spoilt it all, **AS USUAL!** They were supposed to be Bill and Ben the flower-pot men but they suddenly turned into Daleks, chasing everyone round the hall and croaking *Exterminate! Exterminate!* Miss Lamb had to send for Mrs Enderby, head of year.

She hauled them off to her Year Ten Physics lesson where they had to write letters of apology to Miss Lamb and everyone in our class. Ha, ha ha.

18.10. I have made a list of my favourite names for the triplets and stuck it onto the fridge.

GIRLS	BOYS
Anastasia	Jay
Topaz	Jake
Amber	Josh
Rose	Adam
Coral	
Ruby	
Crystal	

Wednesday, 15th December

16.30. We made three-dimensional cardboard stars in Maths. Will hang it on the Christmas tree when we get one. Kerry lost patience with hers. It looked like a squashed octopus. Mia won't be coming to my sleepover after all because Ewan is taking her to the pictures. Narinder looked a bit gobsmacked. She told us later that Mia hadn't said anything to her about not coming to the sleepover. I had a SPOOKY feeling Mia wouldn't come! I think I might be psychic!

Everyone thinks the **Zodiac Girls** is a stunning idea. On duty in the W.Y.P? office at lunchtime. It was a bit sad. Lots of messages from kids who **hate** Christmas because their parents argue about whose turn it is to have them for Christmas. Kids who hate it because they can't stand their step-brother and sisters who come to stay or kids whose parents fight all the time.

I still haven't worked out how I can join *Friends Reunited* without a credit card. Mum would probably let me use hers, but Ian checks the statements every month and he'd want to know why I'd joined and I can't think of a good enough reason. All my friends live in Fletchley!

17.35. Cassie just phoned. She is very upset because her grandad has died. I've invited her to my sleepover. This is **mega spooky**. My horoscope said I WOULD COMFORT A FRIEND!

19.20.

Dear Mum and Ian,

Here are some things I would like for Christmas:

Mobile phone **URGENT!** PLEASE! PLEASE! PLEASE!

A TV for my new room

Or one of those chairs that hangs from the ceiling

Perfume

New jeans

New skirt

Birthday-stone ring (mother of pearl)

Boots (like the ones I showed you in my mag) brown, size 5 1/2 please

Chocolate

Posh soaps and toiletries

An MP3 player

A **surprise** present

P.S. You don't have to buy me **all** of these things. I still want a stocking, please, and I will make a stocking for you to share.

I have stuck my list on the kitchen pinboard.

Thursday, 16th December

17.40. Made mince pies in Food Technology.

Dropped in at Cassie's on the way home. She is still miz about her grandad dying but the pies cheered her up a bit. They were very yummy! So yummy that we couldn't stop eating them! Managed to save one for Mum and Ian to share. Mum was really cross because she'd invited Nolly and Bill to coffee tomorrow and wanted to have the pies for them. Mum has put up her list of baby names.

GIRLS

Lilly
Polly
Rose (after her mum who died when she was twelve).

BOYS

Alex
Morgan
George (after her dad who also died).

Friday, 17th December

8.05. Don't break up till Monday. **What a stupid idea.** What's the point of coming in for one day? Everyone will be mucking about, or playing games that we're allowed to take in. Even some of the teachers can't be bothered on the last day.

16.55. Did Creative Writing in English. Had to write a Christmas story without using the word SAID, and finish it for homework. This is my story so far.

It was Christmas Eve. The triplets Anastasia, Saskia* and Coral were far too excited to sleep. *I hope Santa brings me the puppy I've asked for,* bounced Saskia, who was very excitable. *Calm down,* smiled Coral, the sensible but bossy one. *I can't!* exploded Saskia. *Shut up!* grumbled Anastasia who could be very grumpy when she was tired. *But I'm too excited!* pouted Saskia, who never listened to advice and was rebellious. *I have an idea,* murmured Anastasia, who deep down was kind and creative and loved inventing stories. *Once upon a time,* she soothed, *there were three princesses. Their names were Anastasia, Saskia and Coral...* Her voice droned on. When their parents looked in, the girls were fast asleep. *See how beautiful they are,* sniffed their mother, tenderly. *We are so lucky,* swallowed their father, full of emotion.

21.45. I am worn out. Have spent all evening preparing games and star-sign badges for the sleepover.

*Have added the name Saskia to my baby names list.

Saturday, 18th December,
my **Zodiac Girls** sleepover tonight!
10.20. Just got back from Nolly's computer lesson. Another fiver for my moneybox! Off to the supermarket now in Ian's van to get stuff for my sleepover party.

Sunday, 19th December
16.05. I don't want to boast but that was one of the best sleepovers ever. Actually, I DO want to boast because it was **AMAZING**. First we played the Zodiac game, **GUESS WHOSE STAR SIGN THIS IS.**
VIRGO, Industrious, modest, shy, hard-working at school, neat and tidy and good with money.
FAMOUS VIRGOAN, Roald Dahl.
CORRECT ANSWER, Virgo number one, Cassie! WHAT UTTER RUBBISH! She is the dead opposite! She reckons that she must have been born under Pisces, but adopted by her parents as a baby in August when she was five months old and pretended that she was born in August. This could be spookily true. She's not a bit like her mum or dad.

I have looked up Pisces in my book on star signs. This is what it says:

PISCES, People born under Pisces have the characteristics of the other eleven signs. They are caring and kind but their moods can be very changeable. They make a very good friend, but have little willpower (as in Cassie and chocolate). They like a comfortable life and when down, comfort themselves with food. (TRUE!) One minute they are happy, the next, tearful. (That is SO Cassie!) Can be caring and sympathetic but sometimes led astray by stronger personalities. A Piscean makes a very good and loyal friend because they are kind-hearted.

I was the **only** one that got her right because we've been friends for nearly ten years so I knew that already.

FAMOUS PISCEAN, Elizabeth Taylor.

VIRGO, number two, Narinder! Which is spookily exactly like Narinder! We all guessed her. Easy-peasy.

TAURUS, Reliable, and organised. They seem calm but can get very angry. Can't be rushed and they hate arguments. Often musical and artistic.

FAMOUS TAUREAN, the Queen.

CORRECT ANSWER, Sara. Three of us got that right because she plays the flute in

school orchestra and she's the best in art.
AQUARIUS, Independent. Doesn't like rules. Can be very stubborn. Friendly and generous but not easily taken in and wants proof of things. Wants the freedom to do as they want. Likes to shock. (Dead right!)
FAMOUS AQUARIAN, Charles Dickens.
CORRECT ANSWER, Kerry. Two of us got Kerry right. Sabine thought it was me!
SAGITTARIUS, Sporty, athletic and cheerful. Can sometimes upset people by being too honest and outspoken. Hates sitting still and mood can change quickly from enthusiastic to bored.
FAMOUS SAGITTARIAN, Steven Spielberg.
ANSWER, Sabine. Three correct answers.
CANCER, A good student, always full of curiosity and seeking answers to questions. Good at science, maths and the arts. They follow their own rules. Hard working and likes things to be perfect. Can be stubborn, moody and determined.
FAMOUS CANCERIAN, Lady Diana, the Princess of Wales.
ANSWER – me! Everyone got it right!
After that we played QUEEN CLEOPATRA, invented by me and Cassie. Each of us took it

in turns to be Cleopatra while the others had to be her maidservants for five minutes. Cleopatra lies on the floor and each slave has to moisturise and massage a part of the Queen's body, one each for her feet, one each for her hands and one does a head massage. It was **TOTAL BLISS**. Cassie brought lots of her mum's free samples to use, so we all smelt utterly intoxicating! After a feast of pizzas and ice cream Kerry organised a game called **CONFESSIONS**, where you have to confess to something embarrassing or disgusting that you have never told anyone before.

KERRY confessed that she had once swallowed three tadpoles at junior school because a boy called Rick threatened tell on her to their teacher Mr Smee, for writing I HATE MR SMEE on the blackboard, if she didn't.

CASSIE confessed to biting off her toenails when they get too long. Sara didn't believe that was possible so Cassie did a demonstration and we all felt **sick!**

SABINE confessed to sticking her used-up chewing gum onto her bedside table and it's now fourteen centimetres high.

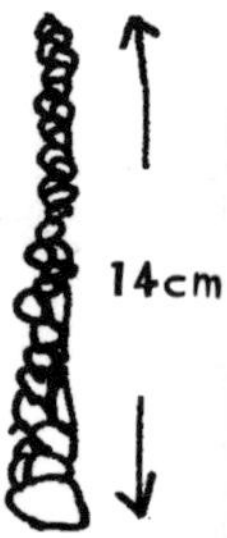

14cm

SARA confessed to sucking all the chocolate off a bag of Maltesers and then giving the sucked sweets to her little brother to finish off.

NARINDER confessed to getting her own back on a boy in junior school, who was always calling her names. She noticed he was scared of crane flies so she collected lots of them in a jar and secretly emptied them into his desk. When he opened it they all flew out and he screamed his head off. No one felt sorry for him because he was a right pain. We were all very surprised that Narinder would ever think of doing something like that. She said, *I don't often get angry, but when I do, just* ***watch out!***

Monday, 20th December

Last day of term!

18.25. It was wet lunchtime today. Kerry had brought in a sprig of plastic mistletoe. She stood on her desk, holding it up for people to kiss under at 10p a go. Soon there was an enormous queue all the way to the Year Eight cloakrooms.

Next thing, Mrs Enderby is standing in the doorway in her silently sneaky prison-warden shoes, bellowing, *What on earth is going on here!* She marched in and snatched the mistletoe from Kerry's hand, saying, *I think I will take that, thank you very much!* Kerry said, *It's all right – it's for charity, Mrs Enderby!* (**Big fib.**) Then in walked Mr Curtis. He looked at Mrs Enderby holding the mistletoe and said, *Well, well Mrs Enderby, you naughty girl, are you looking for a Christmas kiss under the mistletoe?* Kerry said, quickly, *It* ***is*** *for charity, Mr Curtis!* So he put 50p in Kerry's moneybox and gave Mrs Enderby a kiss on the cheek. Everyone cheered like mad and Mrs Enderby went all girly and giggly. She confiscated the mistletoe though, and the money, which we reckon was at least **£7.40**. Gave my presents to Narinder and Mia, friendship bracelets, (£2.50 each). I hope that Mia takes the hint! Also, to Sara and Sabine, (sparkly pink notepad and pen for Sara, purple for Sabine).

This is what I got: homemade fudge from Narinder, a rabbit-shaped rubber from Mia, which I know cost only a mingy **25p** 'cos I bought one just the same last week. From Sabine a sparkly lip-gloss, from Sara a red purse with stars on it. Gave Mr Morris a chocolate orange. He got **eleven** of them!

Went to Jay's after school and looked at the *FRIENDS REUNITED* web page. Haven't registered yet, but Mum's old school is there! I can't wait to get searching! Still haven't worked out how I can get hold of a credit card, though. Just think, this time next year I could be spending some of the Christmas holidays with **my dad!**

Tuesday, 21st December
First day of **Christmas hols**.
11.30. Finished **all** my Christmas shopping!
For JAY, A brilliant joke book, e.g. *What did the policeman say to his belly button?* Answer, *You're under a vest!* **Ho, ho ho!** (£3.25). Also a tube of Lovehearts (28p).
CASSIE, A black belt with studs, **gothic** style (£2.99).
KERRY, A T-shirt with **GET LOST!** printed on it (£2.99).

13.45. Cassie came round. She is distraught. She has found out that on the night of my sleepover her mum had a date with her old school boyfriend! The one she found on *Friends Reunited*! Cass says she wouldn't feel so betrayed and neglected if her mum had **told** her instead of keeping it secret. Cassie knows for certain that her mum secretly planned it all in advance because she had arranged for Cassie's brother, Leo, (a very **spoilt** and annoying eight-year-old), to stay at his dad's flat for the same night that Cassie was at my sleepover. She discovered this when she found a message on the answer phone saying, *Hi there, my little honey bun! Just want to say thanks for a wonderful evening. I feel sixteen again.* His name is Colin Peebles. Worse still, her mum has invited him for Christmas! I told her that I KNOW **EXACTLY** HOW SHE FEELS, because I felt the same when I discovered that Mum was having secret meetings with Ian. I also reminded her that she used to tell me to stop whingeing on about Ian, but she can whinge as much as she wants about C.B. (Colin Peebles), because I understand perfectly what she's going through, and that's what friends are for. I am more experienced in these things and what I have learned is that Ian's OK, and he makes Mum happy. And I'm really excited about the triplets too. So maybe it's not so bad as she thinks.

She snapped, ***Shut up!*** *You're making it* ***worse!*** *I don't want Mum marrying some creep with jumbo ears giving Mum jumbo-eared triplets.*

I calmed her down with my new invention of a chocolate spread and cherry jam sandwich which tastes like Black Forest cheesecake if you close your eyes. She felt much better after. We both agree that it's **unfair** that adults go on at kids for unimportant stuff like a few teeny-weeny guinea-pig poos on the carpet, or being a Goth, or eating all the mince pies when THEY are getting pregnant at seventeen, letting their dogs rule the roost and divorcing. That's the second time I have comforted a friend, just as my horoscope predicted! **FREAKY!** She's going to her grandad's funeral tomorrow. At least her mum won't be able to complain about Cassie wearing her black Gothic look to a funeral.

16.20. Mum had her scan today. They think the triplets are two boys and a girl but they can't be one hundred per cent certain yet. I'm a bit disappointed, but trying not to show it. Cleaned out Twinkle's and Graemella's hutch. Twinkle has invented a new game – hopping on and off Graemella's back. They are **so** cute and funny.

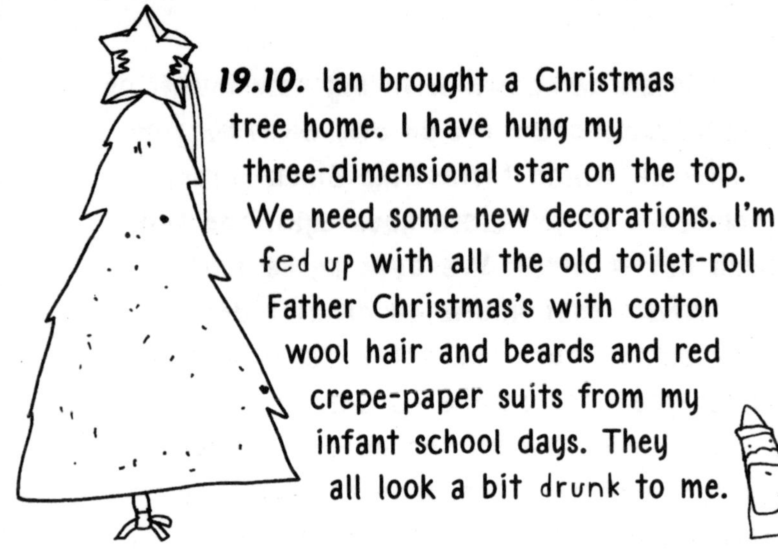

19.10. Ian brought a Christmas tree home. I have hung my three-dimensional star on the top. We need some new decorations. I'm fed up with all the old toilet-roll Father Christmas's with cotton wool hair and beards and red crepe-paper suits from my infant school days. They all look a bit drunk to me.

20.40. Just read through today's diary entry which gave me overpowering urge for another Black Forest cheesecake sandwich. I am eating it in bed. It is SO **YUMMISH!**

Wednesday, 22nd December

18.55. Went round to Jay's this morning with Kerry and Dan. We played Twister and laughed so much we fell into a heap and Dan farted very loudly, which was totally disgusting, but Dan and Jay found it hilarious. I told them how I've found out lots more from Mum about her school days. She was **dead clever** and got mostly A's and B's in her mock G.C.S.Es. It was a real shame that she never got to take them. Her aunt and uncle gave her such a horrible time that she ran away before the exams. Also how I'm just itching to join *Friends Reunited*, pretending I am Debbie Penny, once a teenage runaway, now married and the proud mother of a twelve-year-old daughter, and chatting on-line to her old schoolmates and finding out who remembers my dad.

While I was telling them all this, I could see Jay frowning hard at me, so I said, *Jay, why are you looking at me like that?* He said, *Nothing!* Then shrugged. *Except...* I said, *Look, just **tell me!*** He shrugged again. *Well, I still think that you need to be a bit more sensible about this.* I said, *I am being sensible. I'm one of the most sensible people I know!* And I crossed my eyes, stuck out my tongue, and waggled my ears, saying, *Unlike some people who go round kicking bricks and breaking their toes!* At which point me and Kerry collapsed into hysterics.

Jay sighed, *Yeah, very funny. But – sorry, I still don't think your mum is going to find it very funny! Think about it. How's she going to feel about you digging up some bloke she met at a party thirteen years ago and never saw again? Even if he is your father.* He sounded like some bossy teacher talking down to some stupid little kid! I could not believe what I was hearing. I said, *So you **don't** want to help me then!* He shrugged. I looked at Dan for help. Kerry said, *It's no use asking Dan. He avoids arguments.* I said, *Well, now I know EXACTLY who my friends are! Kerry's on my side, aren't you, Kerry?* She made a sort of 'sorry' face, and said, *Though, in a teeny-weeny sort of way, I do sort of agree with Jay a **titchy** bit.* **I could not believe my ears!** I gasped, *Are you my mate or not!* She said, *Look, don't get me wrong, **I am on your side!** But you don't know very much about your dad, do you? What if he turned out to be a WEIRDO, or HORRIBLE, or maybe a HOMELESS PERSON, OR MAD or just NOT VERY NICE?* I said, *Yeah? But on the other hand he could be a rich tycoon living in a mansion!* She said, *Yeah? **In your dreams!** But it's risky! **Very risky!** RISKY isn't SENSIBLE, is it? And I'd hate to see you getting hurt.*

Dan just sat there flicking through an old *Beano* annual he'd found under Jay's bed. I asked him what he thought. He just shrugged, *Nothing to do with me. It's up to you.* But then he looked up and said, *But I do sort of think that just because something isn't sensible, it doesn't mean it's a bad idea. I mean, what sort of world would it be if everyone was sensible? It wasn't very sensible for Columbus to sail round the world when loads of people thought it was flat, was it? Or to fly to the moon in a rocket. Sometimes you have to take a little risk – as long as you use a bit of common sense. And if I was in Finch's shoes, I'd definitely want to know about my dad.*

I jumped up and gave him a big kiss. I told Jay, *See?* ***Dan agrees with me!*** *I've spent ages thinking about this, and that's what I've decided!* I was feeling really miffed with Kerry too, for siding with Jay. I told Jay, *OK!* ***Don't*** *help me then! I'll manage without you!* I took off the bird brooch that he'd given me and said, *You'd better have this back 'cos I don't think you want to be my boyfriend any more!* He looked gobsmacked. And then I left. Kerry came after me. She said, *Are you mad with me too?* I yelled, ***NO!*** But I was lying. She yelled back, *And don't you* ***dare*** *go kissing my boyfriend again!* And then I came home.

Thursday, 23th December

9.10. I am in bed cringing about yesterday. **I can't believe that I gave my brooch back to Jay!** Even though he was being annoying and bossy! I was revolting to Kerry too. Why am I so **RATTY!**

9.40. My period has just come on.

10.25. Had to wait till Mum and Ian had gone out to phone everyone. I SO need a mobile phone!

11.05. Jay is mad with me for being unreasonable, ungrateful and for kissing Dan. Kerry is mad with me for kissing Dan, also for being mad with her when she was trying to be helpful.
Dan is mad with me for kissing him and making Kerry jealous 'cos she thinks he looked like he enjoyed me kissing him.
I am mad with **myself**.

10.45. Phoned Kerry back and did some **grovelling**. Told her that my period had just come on. She said, *Oh, that explains everything perfectly. OK, I forgive you for* *being a pain in the bum. But you owe me, right? And don't you go kissing Dan again, or else!* She says Jay is dead miz that I kissed Dan AND gave his brooch back! I might have to do some more grovelling.

10.50. Just remembered! My horoscope said that someone would put me under pressure. That someone was **Jay!** It also said, You are searching for something missing from your life. Do not give up. It is within your reach! **SPOOKSVILLE!**

10.35. Phoned Jay. His dad said he was out. Oh, Jay, **call me, please!** If only I had a mobile phone! Life would be so much **easier!**

11.05. Have highlighted **MOBILE PHONE** on my Christmas list in **bright pink** with giant arrows pointing at it and have moved it to the loo door where no one can possibly fail to see it when sitting on the loo.

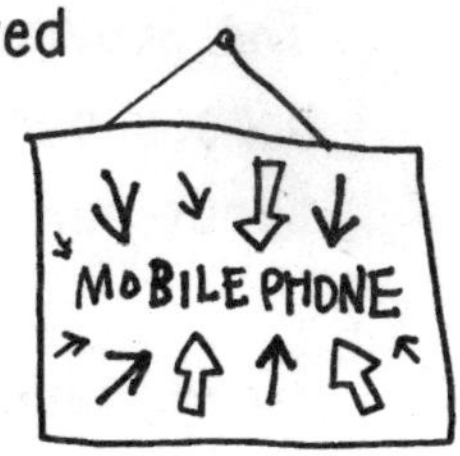

MOBILE PHONE

12.40. Jay came round with a bag of popcorn! And my brooch – which I have pinned on over my heart! I explained that the kiss I gave Dan was only a kiss of friendship. Also that I cannot give up the search for my father because as a Cancerian I just can't help being curious, enquiring, stubborn, moody and **determined**. He said, *Yeah, crabby!* Then he kissed me. It was a very **tickly** kiss. When I put my glasses back on I could see these cute little black hairs growing on his top lip, like a baby moustache! **I fancy him to bits!** He's promised to help me search for my dad and I promised that if we do find my dad, I will tell Mum and make no contact with him unless she agrees. **But what if she doesn't agree?** And what if she does? It's sort of scary either way. I told him about my horoscope predictions. He said, *If you believe that rubbish, you'll believe anything.* It was the perfect way to spend a morning, cuddled up on the sofa with Jay, watching *The Snowman*, eating popcorn, with my bird brooch back on my jumper, and wondering about my dad.

14.15. Mum just threw a **wobbly**, screaming at the vacuum cleaner that it was stupid because it keeps switching off. Then she burst into tears, wailing, *I can't cope with all this* *mess and sawdust! Why did Ian have to start knocking the house to bits before Christmas! I can't even have a shower because the bath's full of floorboards! I've only got* **one** *working socket in the kitchen and it's Christmas the day after tomorrow and I haven't even bought the turkey yet and that stupid Christmas tree keeps falling over and...!* ***Sob! Sob! Sob!*** So I made her lie down on the sofa, and phoned Nolly. She turned up with Bill and we got the place cleaned up while Mum went for a lie down. She said she hasn't been sleeping very well because the triplets play football inside her tum all night. I said, *Or play* ***netball*** *– if they're girls!* Nolly phoned Ian on his mobile and gave him a ticking off, also a shopping list of stuff to get from the supermarket. I ran a nice hot bath for Mum with my posh Shangri-La Bath Serum sample that Cassie's mum gave me. I decorated the tree, and Bill put up the other decorations.

Friday, 24th December
Christmas Eve

11.50. Took my present for Cassie round to her new house. It looks boringly **ordinary** on the outside but on the inside it is SO **COOL**.

The walls and floors are all painted white. It looks **huge** even though it isn't. There are these big paintings of flowers hanging on the walls. Not boringly twee ones, like Nolly has, but giant size, like one HUGE poppy, or one GIANT rose. All the Christmas decorations were silver and white twigs and leaves. Her mum says it is minimalist style. I have changed my mind about my new bedroom. I will have white walls and floorboards instead. Also, a large red comfy dog bed for sitting in with the **Zodiac Girls**, or smooching with Jay. I can easily knock up some giant flower paintings. Cassie's mum is starting up her own beauty salon which will be in one of the bedrooms. She promised to give me a **free** aromatic cleansing facial! The salon will be called OASIS.

14.25. Our flat is now all shiny and clean and the sitting room looks lovely and **Christmassy**. The tree lights are twinkling and the presents are piled up underneath.

15.05. Found Mum crying again. She says she's crying with happiness because we're a real family now and everyone is being so nice to her. She hugged me and said, *I'm so lucky to have you all – and you were the best present I ever had.* I felt totally **horrible** then. A creepy, nasty uncomfortable feeling shivered through me, and I felt so mean that I nearly confessed about *Friends Reunited* and my search for my dad. Instead I asked her, *Mum, do you ever think about my dad?* She cuddled me and said, *Yes, love, I think it's a real shame he doesn't know you. I know he'd be very proud.* I burst into tears then. And so did she. She said, *Just look at us! Two big softies!* I am a **traitor**.

Saturday, 25th December
Christmas Day

8.50. I **LOVE** Christmas!

11.45. Buster is in **BIG** TROUBLE! He's been at the turkey! Mum had left it in the bath overnight to defrost – but SOMEONE used the bathroom and left the door open! We all know it was Bill but he's denying it. Nolly's trying to cut off the chewed bits. Buster's in the garden, howling and scratching at the window.

22.50. Too full up and tired to write. Also a bit tipsy. Too many choccy liquooers. I am wearing my new boots to bed, **I love them SO much.**

Sunday, 26th December
Boxing Day

11.05. Today I am wearing my new jeans (from Ian), my boots (from Mum), my birthstone ring (from Nolly), a matching pendant (Bill) and pink sparkly gloves (Cassie). And Jay gave me a **beautiful** hardback notebook with peacocks on the cover and a box of pens. And in my stocking, furry bed socks, sweets, rabbit-shaped soaps, a mini manicure set, a bath bomb, flowery flip-flops, sweets, lacy pants and – a magic painting book. **I am twelve and a half, Mum!!** BUT...as much as I adore all my presents I can't help feeling VERY disappointed that I did not get a MOBILE PHONE. I **knew** I wouldn't get my own credit card. But I would've swapped **all** my other prezzies, (except my boots), for a mobile! Right now all my mates will be texting away to each other about their presents. I am an **outcast**. I was SO looking forward to chatting in **private** to Jay on Christmas morning. Had to use the kitchen phone to call him but could hardly hear myself think 'cos Ian, Mum, Nolly and Bill were dancing and singing along to 'Rocking Around The Christmas Tree' on the radio.

15.20. Ian said, *Just think, this time next year there'll be three baby boys crawling around on this carpet.* Mum said, *Or three baby girls.* I said, *Or two girls and one boy. Or two boys and one girl.*

Monday, 27th December

21.45. We all went round to Nolly's and Bill's for tea. Watched *The Sound of Music* and sang along. Nolly was Mother Superior, Mum was Maria, I was **all** the Von Trapp children, and Ian was Captain Von Trapp. Bill filled in for all the other singing parts. I laughed **so** much that my ribs ache. I have decided to save up for my own mobile phone from my pocket money.

Tuesday, 28th December

9.05. The strangest thing!! Whenever Ian talks, the triplets start kicking. They don't kick for me or Mum. **Only Ian!**

Wednesday, 29th December

Cassie came round. She says this Christmas was a **huge** improvement on last year, when her mum wasn't talking to her dad and Cassie had to be the go-between, asking her dad stuff like, *Dad, Mum says do you want a turkey leg or turkey breast?* And even though her mum heard him say, *I'd like a leg,* she'd have to tell her mum, Dad says he would like a leg. She said B.E.P. (Big Ears Peebles) came loaded with presents for everyone. A car racetrack for Leo and a **karaoke machine** for Cassie! Her dad was there too with his girlfriend Lindsey. Leo, B.E.P. and her dad spent all day racing on the track and trying to crash each other. Mum took Lindsey upstairs to show her the Oasis Beauty Clinic and gave her a free eyelash dye. After dinner all the grown-ups nodded off, Leo had the racetrack to himself, and Cassie had a **brilliant** time with Lindsey singing along to 'Dancing Queen' on the karaoke. It was the best Christmas since she stopped believing in Santa Claus.

Thursday, 30th December

15.45. I informed Mum and Ian that I am saving up for a mobile. I could not believe my ears when Mum said, *Sorry, Finch, but you're not having a mobile phone until you're sixteen.* I gasped, *You are* ***joking*** *I hope!*

Ian said, *This is not a joking matter, Finch.* I was then was forced to endure a yawn-making lecture from him about the dangers of my young brain being destroyed from the microwaves in mobile phones or something.

I asked, *Oh yeah? So, how come that all my mates with mobiles haven't turned into* ***zombies****, then!*

He said, *Read my lips. You are NOT having a mobile phone until you're sixteen. And you'll be grateful to me one day.*

I yelled, after him, *Yeah, at your funeral!* Mum went **ape** then. I told her, *Fine! You have just ruined my life! I will be Finch-No-Mates then! If that's what you want!* I am sizzlingly, furiously **fuming!**

17.00. THIS IS SO **STUPID!** Anyway, if Ian is right, I won't have any mates left to phone by the times I'm sixteen – 'cos their brains will be zombified! Either way, I can't win!

17.20. Got Mum on her own, went down on bended knees, wept, begged and **pleaded** and went on about being the only one among my mates being forced to live in the dark ages. Soon I won't have any mates! I could see she was having second thoughts. Then Ian walked in saying, *Don't bother nagging your mum. We're united on this!* Thanks a lot! NOT!
HE MAKES ME SO MAD!

17.50. Phoned round all my mates to let off steam. Made sure that Mum and Ian heard every word.

Friday, 31st December

NEW YEAR'S RESOLUTIONS:

1. Join *Friends Reunited.*
2. Find my dad.
3. Start shaving my legs.
4. Experiment with tampons.
5. Stop twiddling my hair round my finger. I thought it looked sort of cute until I saw

a girl on the bus doing it and it looked dead **irritating.**

6. Try to be less bossy with Jay and more feminine but at the same time assertive, alluring and mysterious.

7. Think up a crafty plan to get my own mobile phone.

19.40. Spent the day at Jay's, cuddled up on the sofa watching this old film on telly called *Spartacus.* It was **BRILLIANT!** Spartacus was a real person who was captured by the Romans and made to work as a gladiator. He escaped and led an army of other runaway slaves in battles against the cruel Roman army. The slaves won many battles but eventually the Roman armies captured them. Caesar knew that Spartacus was among them, but didn't know what he looked like, so he promised that he would let all the slaves free if any one of them would identify Spartacus, dead or alive. Spartacus started to stand up, saying *I am Spartacus!* But as he did so, all the other slaves stood up too, shouting, *I AM SPARTACUS!* This was because they loved him so much and wanted to save his life. But the cruel Romans crucified them **all!**

I had tears running down my cheeks. Jay looked a bit wet-eyed too. I've added **Spartacus** to the triplets' names-list. I am staying up to celebrate the New Year with Mum, Ian, Nolly and Bill.

Saturday, 1st January

9.45. Had the weirdest dream. It was like the film *Spartacus.* I was standing before this vast army of men, shouting, *Which one of you is my father!* And they all started calling, *Me! Me! Me!* Then three men stepped forward, shouting, ***NO THEY'RE NOT, I AM YOUR FATHER!*** They were the Prime Minister, Elvis Presley and Mr Sowerbutts! And then I woke up. **WEIRD** or WHAT?

11.05. Each time I see Mum I get this nasty guilty sneaky feeling about my secret search for my dad, and get a terrible urge to blurt it all out and **confess!** So I have shut myself in my room with Graemella on my lap and confessed it all to her. She looked up at me as if to say, *Don't worry, Finch, it's going to be OK*, and licked my hand which in bunny language means **I love you.**

15.20. I wonder what I'll be writing in my diary this time next year. Maybe something like:

Dad has just phoned me on my mobile. Must dash – he's taking me shopping for clothes for our holiday on his yacht in the Caribbean, then on to posh restaurant for lunch. I am dying to ride my new pony, which he gave me for Christmas. He's told me I can invite a friend on holiday. This is SO difficult! Who am I going to choose? Jay, Cassie or Kerry?

Sunday, 2nd January

9.10. Jay just phoned. He said, *Get round here!* ***NOW!*** *I have a surprise for you! And I think you're going to like it.*

17.25. Just got back from Jay's. This has been **A HUGELY IMPORTANT DAY IN MY LIFE** FOR ALL THE FOLLOWING REASONS.

1. I have joined *Friends Reunited*! AND,

registered in Mum's name. And how did I do that without a credit card? Easy-peasy! I borrowed Jay's dad's debit card! Jay told me, *They think I'm sensible enough to borrow it occasionally because it makes it a lot easier when I order books and games on-line.* I gasped, ***What?** You told him porkies! What's he going to say when he gets a bill for joining Friend's Reunited?* He said, ***Two** bills actually, because I've been using the website myself to trace a couple of my dad's old school friends that he lost contact with. It's a surprise for his birthday next week. I'll explain to him that I've been helping you find your mum's old friends. I won't lie to him about it. And I think you should promise me now that you'll tell your mum and Ian before making contact with your father.* I said, *Sorry, Jay, but you're going to have to trust me on this. If you TRULY LOVED AND TRUSTED ME, you wouldn't need to insist on promises.* And I gave him a big kiss and hug, and said, *Sometimes you sound more like a forty-year-old than nearly thirteen!* He said, *Really?* Like he was pleased about it. He's so old-fashioned sometimes. I think this is because his parents are old. His dad is

sixty-three. I don't know how old his mum is.
2. I found Mum's friends!
* Dawn Cooper is a nurse, now married to Gavin Dee. She's expecting a baby in March. She lives in Sidcup, which is not that far from us. It was at Dawn's sixteenth birthday party that Mum met my dad and got pregnant with **me!**
* Daniella Grey is a hairdresser and still lives in Swindon.
* Denise Day is an infant teacher and lives in Hastings.
3. I sent this message to each of them.
Dear Dawn, Denise, and Daniella,
Hello everyone, It's me, Debbie Penny. We were the 4 Ds, remember? This must be a bit of a shock for you after so long – over thirteen years I reckon. You must have wondered why I suddenly disappeared like that and what I've been doing and why I didn't keep in touch. Well, it's a long story and I'll tell you more about it sometime. But I think you all knew what a bully my uncle was and how unhappy I was living there. I just couldn't take it any more. It was just after your sixteenth birthday party, Dawn, remember? My uncle gave me a very hard time about sneaking off to your party. He locked me in my room most of the time. Things

got so bad that when I got the chance, I ran away. I went through some difficult times but a lot has happened since then. I'm now very happily married to Ian, and have a daughter, Finch, age twelve and a half. It was Finch who got me thinking about you all – their class is doing a school project on their parents' school days. That made me wonder what you're all doing now. I wish I'd kept in touch with you all, but like I said, there was too much stuff happening. The other news is that I'm expecting triplets! I've been thinking a lot about you all lately and Finch thought of looking at this website – and here you all are! I've really missed you all. Please get in touch! It would be so wonderful to hear from you all. Love, Debbie.
P.S. All I remember about that party is that I spent most of it with a tall good-looking, dark-haired guy called Tom. Can't remember his surname – what was it?
Love, Debbie (Debbie Tanner now)

Well, I've done it now! I can't go back. My head is swimming with thoughts and emotions. Part of me is SO **EXCITED** that I can't keep still. The other part is thinking, **what if I'm making a big mistake?** What if

Mum is mad about me writing to her old friends? But I don't think she will be. I think she'll be pleased. **And what if I do find my dad?** What if Jay is right and my dad turns out to be horrible and I hate him? What if he's like Mum's uncle? Why did I ever think this was a good idea? Why didn't someone stop me! BUT I CAN'T STOP NOW! **I HAVE TO KNOW!**

Pocket money survey

For the record, this is what Jay gets for pocket money. ***£10* a week and a season ticket for Fletchley United.** His mum buys most of his clothes but he chooses them. He looks after the rabbits and guinea pigs, mows the lawn and empties the dishwasher. He's saving up for a new computer and spends the rest on games, sweets and books. I think his parents spoil him a bit.

22.05. Feel exhausted, but much too excited to sleep.

Monday, 3rd January

17.15. **WOW! WOW! WOW!** Went to Jay's after school and got these messages!

Debbie! This is so wonderful. I have never stopped thinking about you. What happened to you? Why did you disappear like that? We all knew that you had a tough time with your aunt and uncle and wondered if you'd taken off, but we got very worried when we never heard from you. Whenever us three Ds get together we talk about you. I've already told Daniella about your message. Haven't been able to get in touch with Dawn. Please phone me! My numbers are at the bottom of this e-mail. Or can I phone you? Yes, I do remember you dancing with a tall skinny boy but don't know who he was. Sorry. I'm so pleased to hear you're happy. I'm dying to talk to you! All my love, Denise. I'll write more later.

Dear Debbie,
Denise has just texted me about you. This is such fantastic news! I can't believe it. I'm late for work but I promise to catch up later. Give me your phone numbers so that I can call. Here are mine – ring any time. I am so excited to hear from you! I remember that party but wasn't there for long – my dad came to pick me up at ten! It hadn't even got started by then! I can't wait to see you! Speak to you soon, Daniella

Tuesday, 4th January

9.50. Phoned Jay. Still nothing from Dawn. Told him I'm coming over. I'm stressed out from waiting.

16.50. Back home. I'm in my room.
And locked in my drawer is a print-out of an e-mail that arrived from DAWN today! It will go into my scrapbook of **How I Found My Father**. I have another copy, which I have hidden inside my diary.

Debbie! Is it really you? I've just come off duty, checked my e-mail – and there you were! Along with excited messages from Denise and Daniella that you've got in touch. This is so wonderful. I've never stopped thinking about you! In fact my mum and I were talking about you just the other day. She always knew what a terrible time you had with your aunt and uncle, because I told her. She told me that she'd felt so sorry for you that she'd thought about inviting you to live with us. But then, after the party you disappeared. That got her really worried and she was so concerned she reported you missing to the police. They checked it out but came to the conclusion that you'd decided to take off. This is a wonderful way to start the New Year! I can't wait to see you again. Where are you? See below for my address, phone and mob. numbers. Triplets? Blimey! Did you know that I'm expecting a baby too? Due in March. Mum will be so pleased to know you're safe and well. Don't disappear again! I can't wait to see you! Lots of love, Dawn P.S. Tom was my brother Matt's mate, Tom Rix. He and his wife run an on-line sportswear business called TRIX-SPORTS

TOM RIX!
TOM RIX!
MY DAD IS TOM RIX!
I AM FINCH RIX!

I was so **excited** I couldn't stop jumping about and squealing my head off. Jay's mum burst in and said, *What **is** going on in here?* I told her, *Jay's been helping me find some of my mum's old school friends. Please don't tell her – it's a surprise.* I don't know **what** she thought was going on! Jay had gone all red. When she left, Jay said, *You can be **so** embarrassing sometimes!* It was such an exciting and important moment that I felt all dizzy and emotional and weepy. I had to ask Jay to do the rest. He typed in **TRIX-SPORTS** and got all the info we needed.

DIRECTOR: Rix, Thomas

DIRECTOR: Rix, Sally

ADDRESS: 25 Park Grove, Streatham

That's only a few miles from here!

I HAVE FOUND MY DAD!

I AM FINCH RIX

IS SALLY RIX MY STEPMOTHER?

I couldn't help jumping up and down and **screaming** again. I called downstairs, *It's all right, Mrs Carter! I'm just a bit excited because I've found something that I thought I'd lost.*

22.05. I've written a letter to my dad.

Dear Tom Rix,

I know this letter will be a big shock to you, but I think that you might be my father. My name is Finch Penny and I am twelve and a half. (My birthday is 29th June.) My mother is Debbie Tanner, but before she was married her name was Debbie Penny. My mum was best friends with Dawn Cooper. I think you were best friends with Dawn's brother Gavin. My mum met you at Dawn's sixteenth birthday party. Nine months after that party I was born. When I was little, my mum told me that my father died in an accident. But six months ago she told me the truth. She told me that she got pregnant at Dawn's birthday party, where she met a boy called Tom, who was tall and dark haired, and I think that is you. She says that I look just like you! I don't look a bit like my mum. Ever since then I haven't been able to stop wondering about you. My mum and Ian don't know that I'm writing to you. I am going to tell them before I post this letter. I hope they won't stop me. This is SO important to me! I'm enclosing a photo of me. Do you think I look like you?

Yours sincerely, Finch

P.S. My mum is five foot four, has blue eyes and naturally blonde hair. Do you remember her at the party?

P.P.S. Please don't worry that I am trying to get you and Mum back together. She is very happy with Ian Tanner, thank you. He's OK. He's just right for Mum.

PLEASE! PLEASE DON'T IGNORE THIS LETTER.

I have read this letter through seven times. I can't think any more. **I don't know what to do!** I keep thinking, **what if...** And there are so many **what ifs** that I've lost count. I've been going over it in my head for **three hours!** My worst four **WHAT IFs** are:

1. What if it's a big shock for Mum and the babies are born too soon?
2. What if it brings back memories of the bad times and she gets depression again?
3. **What if I'm making a big mistake?**
4. What if Jay is right and my dad is horrible and I hate him?

I'm not going to let myself think about any of that any more! It's too depressing. All I want is to give Mum a nice surprise and make her **happy**. I want her to be happy about finding my dad too. I think I'll tell Ian first. He'll be home soon. How am I going to ask him with Mum not overhearing?

23.40. Ian knows. I went downstairs to get a drink. Mum had gone to bed. Ian was watching telly, so I sat down.

He said, *Shouldn't you be in bed?*

I said, *Actually, I need to talk to you about something very important! I think it might make you mad with me, but I have to tell you. And I want you to promise that you won't interrupt or say anything until I've finished.*

He said, ***Blimey!*** *You've got me worried now! Just tell me!*

So I started telling him how me and Jay had found some of Mum's old school mates on *Friends Reunited*, and I showed him the messages they'd sent.

He didn't say anything for a bit, just sat there reading them. Then he said, *You know what, Finch? This is the best present you could give your mum. Ever since you got her talking about her old friends she's never stopped thinking about them and wishing she'd kept in touch. You must have gone to a lot of trouble.*

I said, *Jay helped me.* Then before I could stop myself, I was blurting, *But that's not all! And I'm not sure you're going to be so pleased about this bit! But I think I've found my dad too!* And it all came spurting out.

He burst, ***Bloody hell, Finch!*** *Any more surprises?*

I said, *Yes. I've written him a letter.*

His eyes nearly popped out. He bellowed, *YOU'VE DONE* ***WHAT?***

I told him. *Calm down! Don't panic! I haven't posted it yet. I don't want to upset Mum, but this is really important to me. I just thought I'd better tell you both first.* And I gave him the envelope with my letter to my dad inside.

He snorted, *And what am **I** supposed to do with it!*

I said, *I want you and Mum to read it. And I'm hoping that you'll let me send it.*

He said very slowly, *Finch, you have got to be joking.*

I said, *I'm **not** joking! It's really important to me. **Pleeeeease!***

He snapped, *Well, I can give you the answer to that right now! **No!*** And he shoved it in his pocket. I tried to speak but he glared, *I don't want to hear another word about this! You hear! **Not another word!***

I pleaded, *But you haven't even **read** it!*

He barked, *I don't need to read it. That's enough! And I don't want to hear any more. Go to bed!*

22.45.

I HATE HIM I HATE HIM I HATE HIM

Wednesday, 5th January

9.55. So much is happening. I'm feeling very emotional and exhausted. Ian woke me up at **half past six** this morning! He had my letter to my dad in his hand. I'd had hardly any sleep, and I felt even more angry with him. He started, *I'm sorry, Finch but...*

So I yelled back, *You're not a **bit** sorry! I don't know why I even bothered asking you!*

He sat down on my bed, saying, *Listen to me first!*

I burst, *GO AWAY! GET OUT OF MY ROOM!* I tried to kick him off, hissing, *I knew you wouldn't understand! I don't know why I even bothered showing you!* And I pulled my duvet over me, like a tent, repeating, *Go away – I hate you – GO away – I hate you – Go away – I hate you – Go away – I hate you...*

Then I heard him say, *Listen, Finch. Maybe I was a bit hasty. You might be pleased to know that I didn't get much sleep last night. But I read your letter. It's a good letter. I did a lot of thinking too, and I realise how much it means to you. And I think your mum will understand that too.*

I told him, *You'd better be telling me the truth. I'll be **SO mad** if you're lying to me.*

He said, I *promise I'm not lying to you. And I'm sorry about what I said last night.* So I peeped out of my tent. He said, *How about we give your mum her breakfast in bed, and you can show her your letter? Let's see what she thinks, eh?* I couldn't say anything for a second. He said, *You could start with the messages from her old school friends. And maybe afterwards would be a good time for you to show her the letter you've written to your dad. How does that sound?* I jumped up and gave him a **big hug** and then I burst into tears. He got a bit emotional too.

We made Mum a breakfast tray with her favourite stuff. Pineapple juice, yoghurt with honey, Marmite on toast, a cup of tea and a red paper napkin left over from Christmas, with golden angels on it. She was still half asleep, rubbing her eyes and mumbling, *What's going on? It's not my birthday, is it?* Ian said, *Not quite, but Finch has got a big surprise for you – a sort of present.*

Mum sat up, all sleepy-eyed. I gave her the **surprise**, a tube-shaped parcel wrapped in angel napkins. Rolled up inside were the

Friends Reunited messages from Dawn, Daniella and Denise. When she found them she started shrieking, ***Oh, Finch, oh Finch! I can't believe it.*** *Did you do this? This is better than all my birthdays rolled into one!* I told her everything, all about *Friends Reunited* and how much Jay had helped me. She sat there, reading them out and sniffing and looking at me. Then she got out of bed saying, *I've got to call them! I want to call them now!*

Ian burst, *Hold on, Debs! Hold on! Finch has something else to tell you. You'd better get back into bed. You might want to lie down for this one.*

She said, *Oh my God! What else have you done?*

Part of me wanted to blurt out everything about my dad, the other part of me wanted to run away and **all** of me was shaking with nerves! I told her, *Well, it's another surprise.* Then I took a big breath and said, *I think I've found my dad. And I've written him a letter.*

She stared at me and said, *Please, please, please, Finch! Tell me that you are joking!*

I said, *I'm not. But don't worry, I haven't*

posted it yet. I want you to read it first. I promised Jay I would. And she read it. I could see tears in her eyes, and they rolled down her cheeks. And when she'd finished reading it I told her how Jay had helped me and made me **promise** that I showed it to her before posting it. How I didn't **really** have a school project – it was just a way of getting information on her mates and school, so that I could pretend to be her and try to trace my dad. She sat there, frowning, sniffing and dabbing her eyes. Then suddenly she burst into tears. And so did I, sobbing, *I'm sorry, Mum! Are you very mad at me?* She hugged me, sniffing, *Of course not. I'm mad at myself, Finch. I wish I'd realised just how* ***important*** *he is to you!* Then we both started blubbering again.

21.20. In bed.

THIS HAS BEEN A MOMENTOUS DAY IN MY LIFE. I HAVE POSTED MY LETTER TO MY FATHER. TOM RIX.

Mum wrote a letter to him too. I made a photocopy of it for my scrapbook, **HOW I FOUND MY FATHER**.

This is a copy of Mum's letter.

Dear Tom,

I can't imagine how you will feel when you read this letter from Finch. It is as much of a surprise to me as it will be to you that she has been trying to find you. The work she has put into tracing you only goes to show how important you have been in her life, even though she has never met you. She only learned the facts of her conception in August last year. I am sorry to say that I have little memory of Dawn's party, only that you were tall and dark, your name was Tom and that we did a lot of dancing and you made me laugh. Somehow, with very little information, Finch has managed to track you down. I am very proud of her. She is a wonderful daughter and I love her to bits. I hope that you can be as proud of her as Ian and I are.

I hope that your wife will understand too. Please, for Finch's sake, phone, write or e-mail so that we can all arrange to meet you somewhere. This is very important to her.

Best wishes,

Debbie Tanner

And she sent our home phone number, both their mobile numbers, and the e-mail address. We have sent the envelope by Recorded Delivery because they are **V.I.Ls** (**V**ery **I**mportant **L**etters). Since then Mum's been nattering **non-stop** on the phone to her old school mates, Dawn, Daniella and Denise, laughing and crying at the same time. It's all getting very emotional.

Thursday, 6th January

7.15. **Begged** Mum to let me stay off school so that I can hear my dad's voice if he phones here. How can she expect me go to school with this dark cloud of anxiety hanging over me all day? I HAVE TO BE HERE! **He could be reading my letter right this minute!** He might phone – **ANY SECOND NOW!** Mum's feeling nervous about talking to him, so why doesn't she let me stay off school? She keeps saying, *It's thirteen years ago, Finch! I only knew him for a few hours!* Then I had the idea of leaving the answer phone on all day. That way, Mum doesn't have to answer the phone, and I get to hear his voice. Late for school now! THIS IS WHEN I NEED A MOBILE PHONE! Don't care if I'm late for school anyway. I am so wound up that I think I might **EXPLODE!** What if he **never** replies? What if his wife won't let him make contact? What if he's chucked my letter in the bin?

15.25. Rushed home from school. **My dad had phoned!** I heard his voice! He said, *Hi, this is Tom Rix. I got your letter. This is a bit of a shock – especially for my wife. We need to talk about this as soon as we can. My wife suggests the café at the Horniman Museum, it's convenient for all of us. How about ten thirty on Saturday? Let us know.* And he left a phone number and a mobile number.

I AM GOING TO MEET MY DAD!

I've already told Jay and all my mates. I told Jay, *I OWE YOU **LOTS!***

Got a detention slip for being late. Got another one from Mr Sowerbutts in Geography for texting a message on Jay's mobile to Mum asking, *Tom phoned yet?*

Friday, 7th January

8.50. I'm all mixed up, excited, scared, worried and I feel **sick**. I have put out my clothes ready for tomorrow, my black jeans, boots, pink velvet jacket and my fave pink and black stripy jumper.

23.00.

Saturday, 8th January

8.50. TODAY IS ONE OF THE **MOST IMPORTANT DAYS IN MY LIFE!**

In about one hour and ten minutes I'll be meeting my dad for the first time **ever!**

HOW AM I FEELING? **NERVOUS! EXCITED! TERRIFIED! SICK! SHAKY!** I'm **so** shaky that it's hard to write. Nothing seems real. **I feel like I'm in a dream.** I wonder how he is feeling.

14.45. **I've met my dad!** I've actually met my dad! **I'VE NEVER FELT SO NERVOUS IN ALL MY LIFE WHILE WE WERE WAITING IN THE CAFE!!** Mum was so twitchy that she spilt her tea. I couldn't take my eyes off the door. Every time a couple walked in I was thinking, *Is this them?* A tall skinny man with dark dreadlocks walked in with a kid in a pushchair. I thought, *OK, he looks cool.* Then I noticed a woman in horrible leopard-skin trousers with a bloke covered in tattoos, and piercings. I was praying, PLEASE, PLEASE! Not **them!**

Then suddenly, **there they were!** I **knew** it was them! They were wearing matching fleece jackets that I'd seen on their website catalogue. And the man was tall with long legs like me, and the same nose and eyebrows and the same shaped face with high cheekbones.

I felt all these tiny shivers going through me. And I knew **for certain** that he **was my dad**. And I got that weird feeling you sometimes get when you wake up in the middle of a dream and you're not sure if you're awake or still in the dream.

I looked at Mum and knew that she'd recognised him, even though she's made out she couldn't remember exactly what he looked like.

They stood there looking round for us and suddenly the woman saw me. She stood staring, almost glaring at me, then she nudged the man (my dad), and they both seemed to stand there, for what seemed like **ages**, staring and talking, like they were discussing whether we were the family they were looking for. But it was probably only a minute or so. They started coming over, and the woman said, *Hi, I'm Sally. This is Tom – and I think you must be Finch – you* *look just like your photo.* They took off their fleeces and sat down. It didn't feel real but at the same time it felt much too ordinary. Ian was saying, *Can I get you some tea or coffee?* They spent **for ever** deciding on scones or tea-cakes. All I could do was just stare at my dad, my head going, *This man is my dad. This man is my dad. This man is my dad...* I don't know how they could **think** about eating. Mum and Sally didn't want anything either. Mum looked so nervous.

When we were all sorted at last, Ian started on about the problem we had finding a **parking space!** I wanted to scream, ***Hold on!*** *This is supposed to be the most momentous day in my life. I don't care about stupid parking problems.* I thought I would **EXPLODE!** So I took a deep breath, looked at Tom and said, ***Excuse me, but I need to know if you think you're my dad or not,*** only it came out a bit louder than I meant it to and lots of heads turned to look us.

Tom nodded, *You're right, Finch. That's why we're here, isn't it? But to be honest, I don't remember much about that party.* He looked at Mum and shrugged, *Sorry.*

His wife Sally said, *This is all a bit of*

a shock to us, as you can imagine, and gave her husband a look. He nodded like he was agreeing with her. She said, *We've talked it over and decided that the only way we can really sort this out is by D.N.A. testing. I found some information on the internet.* She took some papers from her bag and put them on the table in front of Mum, saying, *It's quite expensive, I'm afraid, but it's the only way of being certain whether Tom is Finch's father or not.* She looked at me and said, *Don't worry, Finch. It won't hurt. It's just a swab test from the inside of your mouth. You do it yourself and send it to the laboratory.* Then to Mum and Ian, she said, *You should get the results after seven to ten days or so.* It was like she was a nurse and I was a **patient** or something!

Then Tom looked at me and said, *But the real question, Finch, is can you do this?* And he put out his tongue so that it touched the tip of his nose. Ian stared at him as if he was bonkers. I started to laugh – I couldn't stop. I think it was because I was so nervous and tense. Mum and Ian started laughing too, but Sally snapped, *Tom, can you please be serious for once?*

I managed to splutter, *Sorry, but that is really* ***so weird!*** *Because I'm the* ***only*** *person I know who can do that!*

Then no one said anything for a bit until Sally looked at me and asked which school I went to and what my favourite subjects were and the usual boring sort of stuff. Then Ian asked them about their sportswear website for a bit. And Sally asked Mum about the triplets and when they were due. And all the questions I was dying to ask had to stay inside my head, because sitting there in the café with Mum and Ian and Sally just wasn't the right place. And then they left. Mum looked at me and said, *Well, you can tell who's boss in* ***that*** *family, all right! I'm certain that's your dad, Finch! He made me laugh the first time I met him. Looks like he's still a bit of a joker.*

I said, *He's just like you described him, Mum. But how did he know that I could touch my nose with my tongue!?*

Mum said, *Perhaps it runs in the family.*

Ian was reading the print-outs about blood tests. He went, *Bloody hell! Do you know what this test costs? Nearly* ***two hundred quid!***

Since we got home, Mum and me have been nattering about it non-stop. She says she's

pleased in a way because she still feels bad about letting me believe that the photo of the man on the motorbike was my dad and making up the story of him being killed on the building site. She said, *He's definitely your dad, Finch. He hasn't changed that much. It's a waste of money doing tests if you ask me. Anyone could see how alike you are.*

She's right. We've got the same colour eyes, green – with little gold flecks! I noticed that his hair grows the same way as mine, in a sort of swirl at the top of his head, and our hands are the same with long fingers. I am **ABSOLUTELY CERTAIN** THAT TOM **IS MY FATHER!** Mum says she **KNOWS** he is.

I should have asked to see his feet! Mine aren't a **bit** like Mum's plump little feet. They're long, narrow and bony and pointed.

I bet his are the same. Sally was very **bossy!** But she was also being so polite I couldn't tell what she was really thinking about at all. She was acting like she was at a business meeting or something! It must have been **a major SHOCK** for her when she read my letter!

I wonder what Tom thinks about me? When we got home I phoned Jay straight away. Told him that my dad isn't horrible or a weirdo.

He's **nice** and I really DO look like him – and that he can do that thing of touching his nose with his tongue. I said, *Thanks Jay! I couldn't have found him without you! I owe you a million kisses!* Kerry and Dan were there too. Could hear them all cheering. Kerry will phone later for a gossip about it. I'm going to make a thank-you present for Jay. It's a book of **promises** and looks like a cheque book. Each cheque is a different promise, which he can cut out and claim from me any time he wants. My **promises** are:

Cheque **one**, a liquorice kiss.
Cheque **two**, a visit to the **Ice Cream-Dream Machine**, which I will pay for.
Cheque **three**, a head and shoulder massage.
Cheque **four**, a homemade Black Forest cheesecake sandwich.
Cheque **five**, a **blank** cheque that Jay can write for himself.

18.40. Ian has ordered the D.N.A. swab test on-line ALREADY!

20.10. Mum and Ian are watching telly so have been on the kitchen phone to Kerry with all the news about meeting my dad and Sally.

Also told her about the cheque book of **promises** I've made for Jay. She thinks it's a **brilliant** idea and is going to make one for Dan. I hope she makes up her own promises and doesn't copy mine.

Sunday, 9th January

19.20. Nolly and Bill have been here all afternoon. They wanted to know **everything** about meeting Tom and Sally. I demonstrated how I could touch my nose with my tongue. Ian looked at the TRIX-SPORTS website. He was going, ***Bloody hell!*** *Two hundred quid for a fleece! I can get one down the market for a tenner!*

Here's a print-out from the website.

Welcome to TRIX-SPORTS

We hope you enjoy browsing our new rang of sports and outdoor wear. All our product are made of the highest quality material We have been successfully designing an marketing high-specification yet stylish spor and outdoor wear for seven years now, and th company has gone from strength to strengt Tom Rix designs all our ranges and Sally R manages the commercial and production side the business.

20.20. Came to bed early. Been feeling **hyper** all day, my head is bursting with questions, like, what does my dad think about me? **I thought he was great!** He made me laugh. He's so laid-back and funny. Sally was the dead opposite! What does *she* think about all this? She was polite but to me it must have been a **major** shock for her when she read my letter. I couldn't tell what she was thinking at all.

And what will my name be now?

1. Finch Olive Penny-Rix–Tanner (F.O.P.R.T.)

2. Finch Olive Penny-Tanner-Rix (F.O.P.T.R.)

3. Finch Olive Rix-Penny-Tanner (F.O.R.P.T.)

4. Finch Olive Rix-Tanner-Penny (F.O.R.T.P.)

5. Finch Olive Tanner-Penny-Rix (F.O.T.P.R.)

6. Finch Olive Tanner-Rix-Penny (F.O.T.R.P)

I can't decide!

Monday, 10th January

7.40. Took ages to get to sleep last night. I am worn out from thinking.

MUM IS **TWENTY-FOUR WEEKS** PREGNANT TODAY. I felt her tummy and said, *Can you hear me in there? Is there a baby girl in there?* And one of the babies gave a great big **kick!**

17.55. Called at Cassie's on the way home. Showed her my cheque book of **promises** for Jay. (It's not quite finished yet.) She thinks it's **brilliant**. She hasn't got a boyfriend at the moment but she's going to make a cheque book so she's prepared for when she does! Told her all my news about meeting my dad and did my famous impression of Sally's, *Can you be serious for once?* I'm glad my dad isn't serious. I have enough seriousness from Ian, thank you very much. Cassie says her mum's been seeing a **lot** more of B.E.P. lately, and he comes round far too much. Leo thinks he's great because he always brings presents. Cass likes the presents but not

B.E.P. very much. She thinks he's a bit of a wimp – and a bit **scared** of her! He has some very irritating habits too, like saying, *And how's my Cassie today?* She told him, *I am NOT your Cassie, thank you very much!*

Don't ask me what happened at school today. I wasn't really there. I was designing my new range of outdoor wear for twelves to teens for **TRIX-SPORTS**. They are quite brilliant! Unfortunately Mrs Summerby didn't agree when she found me sketching them in my French exercise book. I have to pay for a new one. Nearly finished my cheque book of **promises** during double Physics. Kerry is going to make one for Dan. She's sworn to secrecy about it as I want it to be a big surprise for Jay!

20.05. I have come to bed early. Exhausted from telling everyone at school about my dad and Sally, and demonstrating how I can touch my nose with my tongue. No one else could do it!

Tuesday, 11th January

8.05. My swab-test kit has **arrived!** No time to do it. Will come home for lunch.

16.45. Posted my swab-test samples on my way back to school at lunchtime. Just finished making my cheque book of **promises** for Jay! Will give it to him tomorrow.

Wednesday, 12th January

Day 1 waiting for D.N.A. test result.
16.50. Jay was SO chuffed with his book of **promises!** Dan is jealous. Kerry told him that if he wants one he's got to earn it first, so he's going to let her copy his chemistry homework.

Thursday, 13th January

Day 2 waiting for D.N.A. test result.
16.10. Boring day. I cannot stand this **WAITING!** I wish I could be put to sleep and woken up when the results arrive. Why won't Mum let me stay home? It's a waste of time going to school. I can't concentrate for a second! In fact I don't remember a **single** lesson we had today!

Friday, 14th January

Day 3 of endless-endless-endless waiting.
16.15. Had double Maths and R.E. today. What's the point?

Saturday, 15th January

Day 4 waiting, waiting, waiting...

18.00. Jay came round this morning. He wanted to cash one of his **promises**. He'd filled the blank one in with...KISSING WITH **TONGUES**. Had to go behind the little shelter in the park to do it in case Mum or Ian walked in. It was TOTALLY **YUCKY! Really-really-really** wet and slurpy and disgusting! He thought it was **brilliant** though. He went all red and sweaty! I won't make any blank cheques again! Met up with Kerry and Cassie at the Mall this afternoon. Told them about the kissing with tongues with Jay. Cassie was squirming, *Don't! Don't, you're putting me off my raspberry and apricot smoothie. I think I'm going to be sick!* Kerry says she'd like to give it a go with Dan! She'll let us know what she thinks about it. She's still making Dan's cheque book of **promises** and she's going to practise **tongues** on her arm. There were **loads** of sales on today. It's so great having pocket money to buy my own clothes! Bought some bunny bed socks, reduced to 50p, furry pink ear-warmers, 99p, and narrow-leg jeans, £5.90.

Sunday, 16th January

Day 5 waiting. Seems like five **years**. Spent all day painting and decorating the triplets' room. Nolly and Bill helped too. Showed them my impression of Sally's, *Tom, can you be serious for once?* Mum said, *I can't help feeling sorry for her though, it must be quite a shock. I wouldn't like to be in her shoes, suddenly having to take on a stepdaughter she never knew about – I thought she was very good about it.* I said, *She's very bossy though!* The en suite bathroom is nearly finished. It's **fantastic**. There's a shower, loo and a bath. The tiles are a lovely bluey-green. It makes you feel you're in a beautiful mermaid lagoon. Nolly cooked dinner, spaghetti with tomato sauce and cheese, then ice cream with home-made chocolate sauce.

Monday 17th January

Day 6 you-know-what...

16.45. Boring day at school. Mum and me overslept this morning. Ian woke me up as usual but I must have fallen asleep again. (Had a very weird dream but can't remember what it was.) Mum had to write me a note – I don't want

another detention slip! I told her to write:
Please excuse Finch for being late for school. It isn't her fault. I am twenty-four weeks pregnant with triplets and needed help with getting out of bed.
Thank you, Debbie Tanner
P.S. We are going through a very stressful time at the moment so please excuse Finch also if she cannot concentrate.

I didn't get a detention!

17.10. I have just remembered my dream!
I dreamt that someone had cut off the end of my tongue and I couldn't reach my nose with it any more. It's so strange what goes on inside you head when you're sleeping.

Tuesday, 18th January

Day 7. Seems more like Day 7,000,000!
***17.00.* Nothing!**
Drama was good today, though. We all had to choose an emotion and act it out for the rest to guess. I did HOPING (hoping that Tom is my dad). They guessed PRAYING or PLEADING or **BEGGING**, which were pretty close ACTUALLY!

Wednesday, 19th January
Day 8 million
8.00. Zilch!

11.50. **THE D.N.A. TEST RESULTS ARRIVED!** Mum sent a text message to Jay during morning break to say that she'd phoned school and got permission for Ian to pick me up and for me to take the afternoon off so that we could open it all together. All the way home I was wishing, PLEASE! PLEASE! **PLEASE! PLEASE!** LET TOM BE **MY DAD!** The result IS...
TOM RIX IS MY BIOLOGICAL FATHER!

Mum says Sally phoned this morning after they got their own letter. They want to meet up again to discuss what to do next. The other **amazing** news is:
1. **They have a daughter!**
2. Her name is Jodie!
3. She's about four months younger than me! I have always **SO** wanted a sister!
4. They have told her about me!
5. They have invited us to their house this evening so we can all meet each other.
6. **I have a half-sister!**

I cannot believe it! That's **two** wishes

which have already come true. **I** AM SO **HAPPY!** I AM FLOATING WITH **HAPPINESS!**

16.20. I have been doing some thinking. If I'm only about four months older than Tom and Sally's daughter, it could be possible that Tom was **going out with Sally at the time Mum met Tom at the party!** And if that's true, Sally must be REALLY REALLY MAD with Tom. I bet she's really mad with **me** too! I don't feel so floaty now.

21.40. In bed. **I** have met my half-sister. It was like looking at myself! We even have the same hairstyle, though I'm a bit taller than her and my chest's a bit bigger. We just stared at each other. Then I remembered how Tom and Sally had stared at me the first time we met in the café. It must have been a **massive shock** for them to see me for the first time!

Ian went, *Blimey! You two could be* ***twins!***

Mum kept saying, *I can't believe what I'm seeing!* I looked at Jodie and gave a sort of friendly, this-must-be-a-big-shock-for-you-but-isn't-it-**exciting?** sort of shrug, but she totally blanked me and looked away.

Then Sally said, *Jodie, why don't you take Finch up to your room while Daddy and me talk to Finch's parents? I'll bring you some drinks up in a minute.*

Without a word Jodie turned and left. So I followed her. We went up loads of stairs to her bedroom right at the top of the house. She shut the door then **glared** at me, *Don't think for one second my mother likes you! She's just being polite. In fact, she* ***hates*** *you. So does my father. He doesn't even remember your mother. He wishes you'd all* ***get lost****. Just because your mother had sex with him doesn't mean you're part of this family. He says he must have been drunk. My mum feels a bit sorry for you, that's all. She's just acting being nice and friendly, but you've caused nothing but arguments.* ***They both wish you'd never been born!*** *That's all I'm going to say to you. Got that?* Then she turned her back on me and plonked herself down at her PlayStation and started playing Dance Mat, like I wasn't there!

Then Sally arrived with a tray of drinks and crisps, saying to me, *I hope Jodie's looking after you.* So I behaved like little-goody-two-shoes, and smiled, *Yes, fine thanks, she's showing me her games.*

After Sally left, Jodie **glared** at me then went back to her game. A few minutes later, her mobile rang. I heard her saying, *Yeah, she's here now. Yeah, I might do that. Hold on – I'll have a look.* She swivelled round on her chair, looking me up and down like she was inspecting me and said into her mobile, *She's wearing cheap-looking jeans and a* ***tarty****-looking top.* And I realised she was talking to her friend about ME! I was SO MAD! But I wasn't going to let her see how **stupid** I felt and upset and angry and disappointed or that I even cared! 'Cos I knew that's **exactly** what she wanted! But I wasn't going to stand there listening to her rubbishing me either! And I couldn't walk out and go downstairs to Mum, complaining that she was being horrible to me, could I? Anyway, I wanted her to know she couldn't push me around! So I ignored her and started to explore her room. That always winds me up if someone pokes around my room without asking. And I wanted SO MUCH to annoy her. But she carried on deliberately ignoring me. Even so, I made a point of taking no interest at all in the wall of boring exam certificates for ballet and piano and violin and stuff. What a smug little **show-off!**

Her room was **huge** with lots of alcoves and cupboards. She kept her back to me, nattering away to her mates and giggling.

I bet she'd told them to phone so that she didn't have to talk me. She was trying so hard to wind me up but I wasn't going to let her win so I carried on exploring. I could still hear her but I couldn't **see** her 'cos there were these big beams and a sloping wall in the way. I peeked into one of the cupboards – which turned out to be an **en suite bathroom!** It was all pink and white with a shower and loo and one wall was this **huge** mirror! I heard her saying, very loudly on purpose, *No, unfortunately she's still here! I think she's beginning to get the message though!* The next cupboard was a wardrobe, full of Jodie's clothes. Stuff I would have died for! There was this **beautiful** black velvet skirt with coloured beads on the hem in red and turquoise and jade. I matched it up with a turquoise top and a little black suede waistcoat with fur edgings and some red suede boots. Jodie was still so busy yapping and laughing into her mobile and deliberately ignoring me that she didn't even notice me nipping into her en suite to try them on. I decided to make her notice by starting on the drawers, pulling stuff out and making loud remarks like, *That's a definite NO-NO*, and, *Wouldn't be seen **dead** in that! This is cute! Can I have it? But these trousers are vomit-making! Yuk!* That made her take notice all right. She spun round on her chair with her phone still glued to her ear. I posed like a model, saying, *What d'you think then? Gorgeous or what?* She glared at me, like she was too gobsmacked to say anything. But she managed to gasp into her mobile, *Did you hear that! She's only been trying my clothes on! Can you believe that! **Who does she think she is!*** Then she slammed down her

mobile and charged towards me, screaming, ***Take those off! Now!*** I said, calmly, *OK. But you have to ask nicely first.* She looked like she was going to **explode!**

But before she could say anything, there was a little knock on the door and Tom put his head round to say that Mum and Ian were ready to leave. He looked at all the clothes on the floor, then at Jodie, then at me. I said, *Jodie's been letting me try on her clothes, haven't you? Thanks a lot, Jodie, I've had a brilliant time.* Then I nipped into her en suite to change. When I came out, Jodie had gone. Tom said, *So how did you two get on then?* And I said, *Oh, **fine**, thanks!*

Mum, Ian and Sally were waiting in the hall. Sally was being all jolly and bouncy, going on about getting together again so that we could get to know one another better and that she'd sort something out. I wasn't sure if she meant all of us or just me and my dad. What I really want is some time with him on my own.

Tom said, *How about the London Dungeons or something?* I said, *Yeah, **great!** I've never been*

there! And I said it very loudly and excitedly, hoping that Jodie could hear and I could wind her up. All the way home, Mum nattered on about the house and how well off they must be and wanting to know why Sally and Tom hadn't said anything about Jodie when we met at the café, when it was as clear as daylight that I looked just like their daughter. And they must have known that before we met because I'd put a school photo of me in the envelope with my letter. And then Ian went on about how a D.N.A. TEST was the only way to be **one hundred percent** certain and so that was why we had to wait until the tests were confirmed, blah, blah, blah. Then Mum wanted a minute-by-minute account of what Jodie said to me and what I said to her and what I thought about her. So I made it sound as though we'd got on OK, but it had been a bit strange for both of us to meet for the first time – which actually sounded very convincing – even to me! I described her room and her en suite and how she'd let me try on some of her clothes. And Mum looked **so** pleased, I started to feel really guilty about all the lies I was telling her, but I couldn't stop. **Then it got truly**

scary! Because Mum turned to me and said, *Maybe we could invite Jodie over sometime? And when the house is sorted she could stay for a weekend.* So I nodded, but my head was screaming, *I HAVE MADE A **TERRIBLE MISTAKE!** AND THE **LAST** PERSON I EVER WANT TO SEE AGAIN IS JODIE RIX.* But I'm NOT going to give up my dad Tom. **And I'm NOT going to let Jodie win!** And I'm not going to have Jay telling me, *See? I told you it was risky!* I can't help feeling dead jealous of Jodie's room! It had these wonderful big windows in the roof where you could see the stars twinkling in the sky. She's got her own computer and TV too – and one of those chairs that hang from the ceiling! Just like the one I'd wanted for Christmas! (But didn't get!) And a princess bed with lacy curtains. And **none** of her clothes were yucky at all!
I was dead **jealous** of everything!

I **HATE** JODIE!

I HATE HER!

I HATE HER!

I HATE HER!

SHE IS A **COW!**

MOO-MOO!

YOU ARE **NOT** GOING
TO BEAT ME MOO-MOO!

YOU DON'T SCARE ME!

JUST YOU **WAIT** AND **SEE!**

With **thanks** to:
David, computer-whiz and tea-boy.
Annaise, for the low-down on
school and teachers.
Fiona, for all I needed to know
about multiple births.

A big **THANK YOU** to **Mrs Chapman** and **Mr Dunthorne** and **Year Seven** of **Bignold Middle School**, Norwich, for their help with the pocket money survey.

ORCHARD BOOKS
338 Euston Road, London NW1 3BH
Orchard Books Australia
Hachette Children's Books
Level 17/207 Kent Street, Sydney, 2000, NSW, Australia

First published in Great Britain in 2006
A paperback original

A CIP catalogue record for this book is available from the British Library.

ISBN 1 84616 082 0

1 3 5 7 9 10 8 6 4 2
Printed in Great Britain

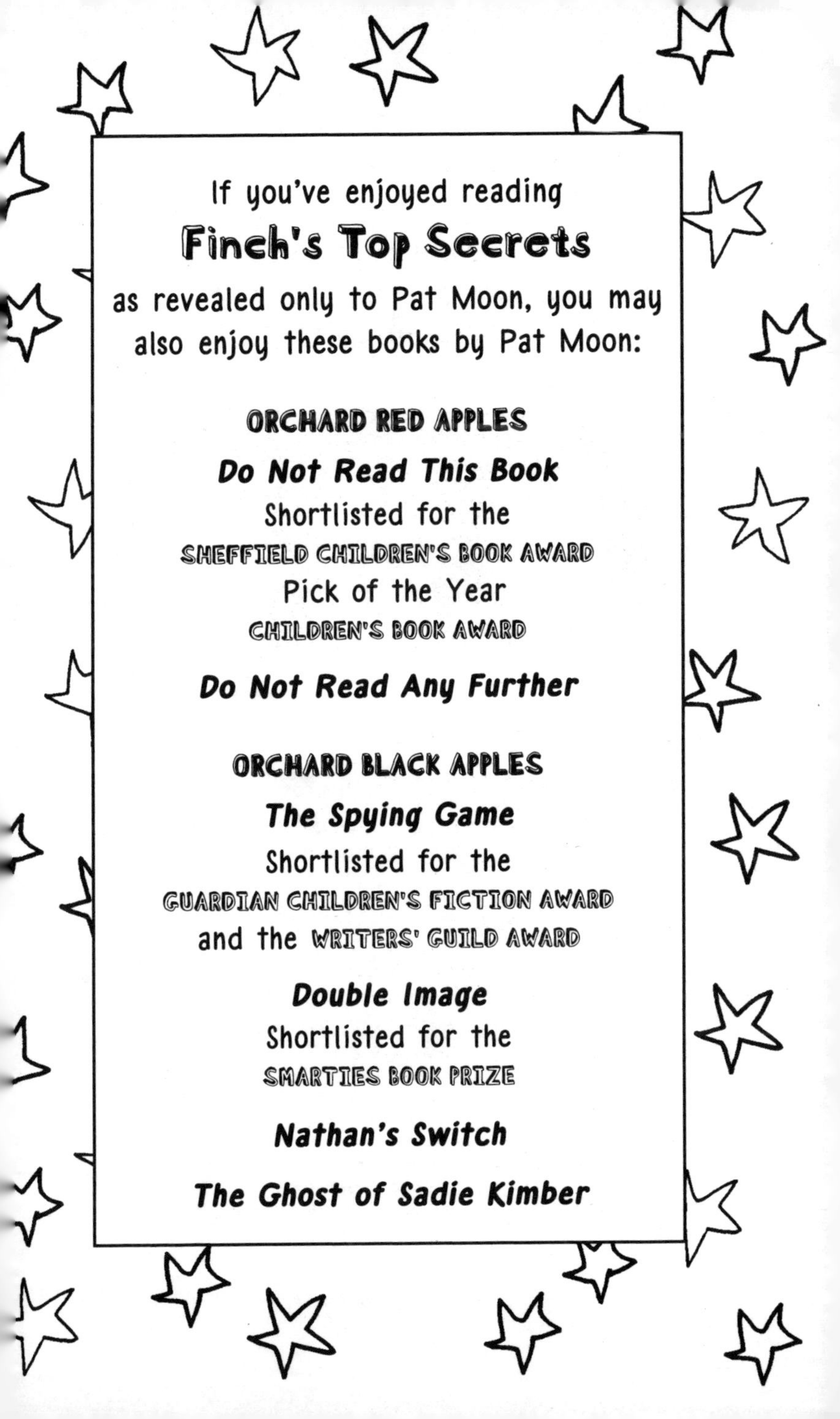

If you've enjoyed reading

Finch's Top Secrets

as revealed only to Pat Moon, you may also enjoy these books by Pat Moon:

ORCHARD RED APPLES

Do Not Read This Book

Shortlisted for the SHEFFIELD CHILDREN'S BOOK AWARD

Pick of the Year CHILDREN'S BOOK AWARD

Do Not Read Any Further

ORCHARD BLACK APPLES

The Spying Game

Shortlisted for the GUARDIAN CHILDREN'S FICTION AWARD and the WRITERS' GUILD AWARD

Double Image

Shortlisted for the SMARTIES BOOK PRIZE

Nathan's Switch

The Ghost of Sadie Kimber

squeak…
squeak
squeak…
squeak
squeak…
squeak
squeak…
squeak
squeak…
squeak
squeak…
squeak
squeak…
squeak
squeak…
squeak
squeak…
squeak

squeak...
squeak
squeak...
squeak
squeak...
squeak
squeak...
squeak
squeak...
squeak
squeak...
squeak
squeak...
squeak
squeak...
squeak
squeak...
squeak

Rave Reviews for

Do Not Read This Book

(also about me, Finch Penny)

"A terrific read"

The Guardian

"A lively and entertaining read and well worth ignoring the title for"

Time Out – Kids Out

"An entertaining and poignant story"

Book Trust

"Although essentially light-hearted, this is a book which delivers"

Books for Keeps

"Told in diary form, this lively, warm-hearted tale has broad appeal"

CHILDREN'S BOOK AWARD, Pick of the Year

Shortlisted for the

SHEFFIELD CHILDREN'S BOOK AWARD